Date: 10/3/17

LP FIC CARTLAND
Cartland, Barbara,
The Earl's revenge

THE EARL'S REVENGE

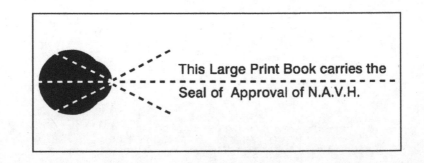

This Large Print Book carries the
Seal of Approval of N.A.V.H.

THE EARL'S REVENGE

BARBARA CARTLAND

THORNDIKE PRESS
A part of Gale, a Cengage Company

Farmington Hills, Mich • San Francisco • New York • Waterville, Maine
Meriden, Conn • Mason, Ohio • Chicago

LIBRARY OF CONGRESS CATALOGING-IN-PUBLICATION DATA

Names: Cartland, Barbara, 1902–2000, author.
Title: The Earl's revenge / by Barbara Cartland.
Description: Large print edition. | Waterville, Maine : Thorndike Press, 2017. | Series: Thorndike Press large print gentle romance
Identifiers: LCCN 2017014796| ISBN 9781432841812 (hardcover) | ISBN 1432841815 (hardcover)
Subjects: LCSH: Large type books. | GSAFD: Love stories. | Regency fiction.
Classification: LCC PR6005.A765 E17 2017 | DDC 823/.912—dc23
LC record available at https://lccn.loc.gov/2017014796

Published in 2017 by arrangement with Cartland Promotions

Printed in Mexico
1 2 3 4 5 6 7 21 20 19 18 17

*"True Love can never be
changed or lost
by the passage of time, old age
or death."*
Barbara Cartland

CHAPTER ONE:
1819

Charles Lyndon was driving his Highflyer phaeton.

He thought his team of four horses were the best he had ever handled.

This build of phaeton was becoming most popular with the young bucks of St. James's. It was an immensely high vehicle and extremely difficult to drive particularly with four horses.

The rear wheels were unbelievably five feet eight inches in diameter and the floor of the body was five feet from the ground.

Charles Lyndon had owned his Highflyer since he had returned from the Army of Occupation in France.

He considered it was the most sporting vehicle any gentleman could possess, as it lent itself to racing and there was always the chance of an accident which might prove fatal.

The young bloods found this most alluring.

The vehicle's great height made it possible for the fashionable ladies of Society to gaze insolently down on the pedestrians.

Charles Lyndon never felt like that, but he was very conscious of his own importance and position.

He was undoubtedly since his return from the war the most handsome, the most sought after and the smartest buck of all the bucks in White's Club.

He had, in fact, taken London by storm.

He had returned from France with two of the most prestigious medals for his gallantry the Duke of Wellington could award in his Army.

He was also the youngest ever Commander of a large body of troops in the British Army.

The Duke had praised him so highly to the Prince Regent that he was a constant visitor to Carlton House.

In addition he was extremely rich, not only because his father, who had died, had left him a large fortune, but his mother had been a great heiress.

To crown it all he was heir presumptive to his uncle the Earl of Lyndonmore, who had been ill for some years, but had managed to reach the age of sixty-five.

All Charles's friends admired and imitated him, but there were, of course, always a few men who were envious and jealous.

Especially they were jealous of his success amongst the beauties of the *Beau Monde.*

They called him the *'never never Peer.'*

Charles managed to laugh at this,

but at the same time the sobriquet annoyed him.

He enjoyed a year of endless gaiety and festivity in London after his return from France. It was not only the sophisticated married and widowed ladies who would fling themselves into his arms, but he was also pursued by every ambitious mother with a *debutante* daughter.

The Cyprians at the time were at the height of their fame and it was not surprising that he had courted the most beautiful, the most talented and most sought after of them.

His life had become almost too perfect and easy and he found himself at times longing for more excitement and the unexpected as had always occurred at war.

It was this more than anything that made him decide as he was nearing twenty-eight that it was time he was married.

He owned one of the finest houses in England.

Lyndon Hall in the County of Berkshire had been in the family since the seventeenth century.

The old house had been pulled down and while a new mansion was being built, the Earl of Lyndonmore had moved to Northumberland, where he found better fishing and grouse shooting than anywhere else in the country.

He had therefore given over the family house to his brother, Charles's father.

Charles had been brought up at Lyndon Hall and he loved it more than any other place in the world.

The rebuilding of the mansion had been carried out by the greatest architect of the time — Robert Adam.

His genius belonged to the school of architectural thought which sprang from the Italian Renaissance with its virtues of formality and dignity and which had produced a great number of British historic houses and buildings.

Robert Adam, however, was freer and bolder in his approach. His motto was not correctness — but movement.

At Lyndon Hall he achieved this brilliantly with the contrasting curves of a magnificent staircase and he had designed a dome more impressive than on any other house and his unique marble hall was the finest ever seen.

When it was finished the house was larger, more beautiful and more imposing than any Palace.

Once he had decided to make up his mind, Charles always worked quickly.

If, after his father's death he was to live at Lyndon Hall, he required a wife who would naturally in time give him the son, or rather sons, he needed to inherit all his vast possessions on his death.

He looked round Society ballrooms at the eager faces whose eyes lit up whenever he appeared.

He always chose to dance with the most beautiful of all the beauties the *Beau Monde* could produce.

Silver Bancroft was the daughter of a distinguished Statesman.

She was undoubtedly the most admired and the most beautiful of her contemporaries.

Charles had been struck from the first moment he had seen her, but not exactly in love.

He mused about her as his wife and he was seeing her projected against the background of Lyndon Hall.

He was aware she equalled in beauty the sculptured Goddesses who decorated the Marble Hall.

He knew instinctively, without

asking her, what her reply would be if he offered her marriage.

She had received every compliment it was possible to receive and it was said that her more serious suitors were already numbered in double figures.

Charles however was not worried.

He would be the victor as he always had been and why not when it came to matrimony.

Whilst he was dancing with Silver last night he had whispered to her,

"I have a question to ask you and I am wondering where we can be alone."

Silver had laughed.

She had often been told that her laughter was like the sound of silver bells.

It was one of the reasons she had changed her name from Sylvia, as she had been christened, to Silver.

It was inevitable that every man when he heard her name would say, "That is not right for you. You should be Gold or Diamond, nothing less!"

She had smiled at them all bewitchingly and at the same time she thought it would be a pleasant change if any man said anything different to her from the last man.

She knew without Charles saying any more what he intended, so she had replied,

"We will be travelling to the country tomorrow, as Papa likes to be there for the weekends. If you call on Saturday afternoon, I shall be delighted to greet you."

Charles did not say that it would delight him too, so he merely replied,

"I will be with you at two o'clock."

Then to her surprise he did not ask her for another dance and he left the ball a little later without even saying goodnight.

Nevertheless as she returned to her father's house in Belgrave Square she was telling herself she had beaten all her friends.

They had tried to attract Charles Lyndon's attention ever since he had appeared on the Social scene.

Charles drove his horses with an expertise which was exceptional like everything else he undertook.

He was thinking that they should hold the wedding in the country and after a short honeymoon they would go to Lyndon Hall.

There were a great number of improvements that he wished to undertake at the Hall including a large amount of restoration.

The house had been neglected in the war whilst he had been away, although the older servants, who had been there ever since he was a boy, had looked after it as well as they could.

Yet a certain amount of money needed to be spent on redecoration of the main rooms and most of the outside brickwork needed repointing.

'I have a great deal to do,' Charles

told himself, 'so there is no question of being bored. Silver can do all the entertaining that is socially necessary.'

He realised only too well that would be inevitable as once he took up residence again the neighbours would fall over themselves to call on him and many of them had been close friends of the family when he was a boy.

He decided he would build a private Racecourse.

Social life had come to a standstill during the long war with Napoleon, but now that England was the glorious victor everything would return to normal and no one would have a moment to spare.

He had certainly found London

overwhelming.

He had noticed before he left his house in Berkeley Square that there was a huge pile of letters unopened on his writing desk.

They were mostly invitations he felt sure and in a short time there would undoubtedly be an enormous pile of wedding presents.

He was most thankful for his extremely intelligent and bright secretary.

The man who had served his father had retired and he had therefore asked Major Monsell who had been under his command to take his place.

Charles was sure he would soon put all his affairs into order and save him a great deal of tedious work.

The horses he was driving were beautifully trained — he had purchased them at Tattersall's the previous week.

They were now gathering speed and he thought he had never driven a better team and although they had been expensive, they were worth every penny he had paid.

He turned in at the somewhat over-elaborate gates of Lord Bancroft's house.

He felt very certain he had broken every record that anyone else could have achieved in driving down directly from London.

He was also aware that it was exactly three minutes before two o'clock and punctuality always pleased him.

It was one of the virtues he had been noted for in the Army and he was extremely annoyed if any of his men were late on parade.

Or he would be angry if they did not carry out any order he gave them as quickly as he expected.

Lord Bancroft's house was vast and opulent, but not particularly attractive.

As his phaeton came to a standstill, a red carpet was run down the steps up to the front door and two footmen in ostentatious livery ran to the side of the phaeton.

Charles's groom, who had been seated behind him, now jumped down to go to the horses' heads.

Charles next descended slowly

and with dignity.

This was somewhat difficult considering how high above the ground the driver's seat was situated.

As he walked up the steps the footmen bowed and a white-haired butler greeted him.

"Good morning, sir. I do trust you had a pleasant drive from London."

"Very pleasant and I am sure I set a record."

The butler smiled.

"That's just what we expected, sir."

He led the way along a heavily furnished passage without saying any more and opened a door at the end.

As Charles went in he was aware

that the room was heavily decorated with flowers.

Silver was standing by the window wearing a pink gown.

She looked like a rose herself.

"Mr. Charles Lyndon to see you, Miss Silver," the butler announced in stentorian tones.

She turned away from the window, where she had been looking at the white doves in the garden below.

Charles walked towards her and she held out her hands.

"I thought perhaps you would have forgotten that you were coming here today, Charles."

"You know perfectly well it is something I would not forget," he replied. "And I must tell you that you are looking very lovely today."

She smiled sweetly at him as if the compliment was something she had not heard before.

"I think you know why I am here," he began.

"You said that you wanted to see me, but you did not tell me the reason."

"What reason could there be, except that I want, as I have never wanted anything, for you to be my wife!"

Silver gave a start as if she was surprised and then she murmured,

"How could I have ever guessed that was what you wanted to say to me?"

Charles's eyes twinkled.

"I have never known you to be

anything but most intelligent, Silver, so I am therefore quite sure, as we have been together so much for these last three weeks, that you realised I love you."

"I thought that maybe you did," she answered, "and when you kissed me the night before last, I was certain at that moment that we both felt the same."

"And indeed I felt what you were feeling and this is what I have brought you."

He opened a small box before he gave it to her.

She saw that the box contained a diamond ring.

It was unusually beautiful in that the diamond in the centre was large and bluish white and was surrounded by other smaller diamonds of the same superlative quality.

Silver gave a little cry that could have been either surprise or delight.

Then, as Charles put the box into her hands and his arm went round her, she blurted out,

"Wait!"

"I thought," he told her in a deep voice, "you would have thanked me without words."

His lips were seeking hers, but to his surprise she moved away from him.

Then when she was facing him, she said,

"I am sorry, Charles, but I cannot marry you."

For a short moment there was an astonished silence before he questioned her,

"What do you mean by *that*?"

"I mean that I cannot marry you and thus I cannot accept this very beautiful ring."

Almost reluctantly she closed up the box and held it out to him.

He took it from her automatically.

"I do not understand. You made it quite clear when I kissed you that you felt an affection for me. I thought when I brought that ring for you this morning, there was no question but that you wished to be my wife."

"I did feel like that when we were in the garden, but now things are rather different."

"What do you mean? What are you talking about?"

He was finding the whole conversation completely incomprehensible.

It had never occurred to him for an instant that she would not marry him.

He had kissed her very passionately in the garden of Devonshire House and she had made it quite clear then that she loved him, he believed, to distraction.

He could not understand now what she was saying.

Nor why she had moved away from him.

"This may come as something of a shock to you," Silver continued hesitatingly, "but I have now promised to marry Wilfred Shaw."

For a moment Charles thought he

had not heard her correctly — it was impossible to accept what she had said.

Wilfred, the Marquis of Shaw, was indeed the most unattractive young gentleman.

Most members of White's considered him a pest as he would just force himself on a company of acquaintances who had no wish for him to join them and he would talk incessantly in a high-pitched voice about his grievances with his family or his horses.

He was undoubtedly a bore and, as Charles always thought, an unprepossessing one.

He could not believe it that Silver had actually said she was going to marry Wilfred Shaw.

Then almost as if it was opened in front of his eyes, he saw a paragraph.

He had read it in *The Morning Post* whilst he was having his breakfast.

"His Grace the Duke of Oakenshaw is seriously ill and we understand his relatives have been sent for from all parts of the country. His heir, the Marquis of Shaw, has already departed for the family seat in Oxfordshire where the Duke has been indisposed for some weeks."

Charles had read the paragraph in the paper without much interest.

He thought that Wilfred was likely to be even more of a bore once he became the Duke.

Now as he stared at Silver without

speaking, she stammered a little incoherently,

"I am sorry — Charles if it — upsets you."

"Upsets me!" he exclaimed. "You know perfectly well that you are only marrying Wilfred Shaw for his title. How can you stoop to do anything so despicable?"

Silver turned her lovely face away from him.

"I knew you would not understand," she simpered, "but I want to be a Duchess and you know only too well it may be many years before your uncle dies."

Charles drew in his breath.

He realised without her saying it out loud that she was thinking of him again as *'the never never Peer'*.

He put the little velvet box into his pocket and in a controlled voice which was bitterly sarcastic, he grated,

"Of course I must offer you my congratulations and my good wishes for your happiness."

He bowed and turning round walked to the door.

As he pulled it open, Silver gave a little cry.

"Wait, Charles, wait! I want to talk to you!"

"There is *nothing* to say."

He walked from the room shutting the door quietly and deliberately behind him.

He strode without hurrying down the passage and into the hall.

The butler was not there and the

three footmen in attendance looked at him in surprise as he passed them by without speaking.

Then walking slowly back down the carpeted steps, he climbed back into his phaeton and his groom hurriedly jumped up behind him.

He drove off down the drive.

As he did so Silver appeared at the top of the steps.

He thought she called out his name, but he did not listen and turned his face away so he need not look at her.

He was still finding it so difficult to believe what he had actually heard.

How was this possible?

Silver was beautiful, charming and, he had felt, in love with him.

How could she stoop to marry an unpleasant bore like the Marquis simply because he would become a Duke?

Charles felt as if he had been struck heavily in the face. He found himself not only surprised, but horrified and extremely angry.

He was not only angry with Silver but with himself.

How could he with all his experience have believed that she loved him and would make him a good wife?

All she had been thinking of was to grab the highest title available.

The man attached to it obviously did not matter!

All that mattered was his rank in the Nobility.

Deep down in his heart Charles had always been an idealist where women were concerned.

This was because he had loved his mother, who had been a sweet and lovely person and had adored his father.

She thought that everything he did was perfect and Charles could not remember any disagreeable words being exchanged between his parents. If they had ever disagreed with each other, it was not in front of him.

Because he was an only child, he supposed he had been spoilt. Both by his father and his mother.

Together they had given him the idea that because he belonged to them, he was superior to anyone else.

He had worked very hard at Eton, but he had done so because he wanted to go back to show them the prizes he had won.

They had been delighted with the good reports he received and there was no disguising their joy in the way he excelled both at lessons and at games.

When he had been such a success in the Army, he had always known it was due to his parents.

He had been brought up to accept that he must be an exceptional person because he was the son of two such exceptional people.

They had both died while he was with Wellington's Army.

First his mother died one cold

winter, when many of his men were suffering from frostbite on the mountains of Portugal, and his father had followed her shortly before Wellington's brilliant campaign from Spain into France.

There had been no question of Charles getting leave to go home. He could only write to his relatives.

When his father died too he felt utterly alone and perhaps one day, he hoped if he was fortunate, he would find someone to take his mother's place.

He had been sure he had found her in Silver.

But she had revealed herself as a greedy, grasping snob and had also showed him up as being a bad judge of character.

He should have waited for the real love that he had known when he was a child.

As he drove along the narrow twisting roads he was ashamed of himself.

Never again would he be so foolish as to be blinded by a beautiful face.

Never again would he be tricked into believing that a woman who possessed one also had a beautiful heart.

Then he recognised that having just made a fool of himself he would surely find a number of his acquaintances would think it amusing that he had been deceived.

He had not actually told anyone that he was going to marry Silver, but he knew it was expected, considering they had been together so much in the last few weeks.

This morning when in White's, he had said that he was going to the country and he knew that quite a number of the members guessed why.

They had raised their glasses.

"Good luck, old man," they had called.

He had never anticipated that he might suffer the first big defeat of his life.

It was simply because the old Duke of Oakenshaw, who had never been particularly interesting, was dying.

Charles realised that the ambitious Society mothers would welcome him back with open arms, but his enemies would certainly be so delighted that *'the never never Peer'* had been set down.

Charles wondered what he should do.

When he was back in London no one would believe that he had changed his mind at the last moment and had not asked Silver to be his wife.

When her engagement to the man about to become the Duke was announced, they would be laughing behind their hands.

They would all say that for once in his life Charles Lyndon had received his 'come-uppance'.

'What shall I do?' Charles asked himself.

He could of course go home to Lyndon Hall and yet he felt in a sort of twisted reasoning that would be running away.

He had always instructed his men when they were in battle to face the enemy and fire the first shot.

It was difficult to think how he could do that now.

In fact almost impossible.

He was now nearing the turn onto the main road to London when suddenly he was aware that one of his horses had slowed down.

He pulled the team to a standstill.

His groom guessed at once without being told what was wrong. It was the front horse on the offside.

He examined it, then walked back to his Master.

"I'm afraid, sir, Raindrop's lost one of 'is shoes and there may be summit wrong with 'is leg."

Charles looked around and just ahead he could see a small village with thatched cottages.

"Ask if there is a forge anywhere nearby here," he ordered his groom.

"Very well, sir."

He was just about to open a cottage gate when a man came out through the door.

The groom obviously asked him where there was a forge and he pointed down the road they were on.

The groom came back to report to Charles.

"The man tells I, sir, there be no

forge in the village, but there be one up at the 'ouse us comes to in about fifty yards further on."

"We will go there and if they have the right tools I am sure, Hobson, you can put a shoe on Raindrop's foot."

Hobson did not answer, he merely swung himself into the seat at the back as Charles drove on.

Through the village and fifty yards further on there was a large iron gate with a lodge on either side.

He realised that this was the house he was seeking and drove up the drive.

At the end of the drive there was a large attractive house which appeared somewhat dilapidated. There were cracks in many of the windowpanes and tiles missing from the roof.

The only thing that mattered, Charles thought, was that they had a forge and that it was in working order.

He pulled the horses up outside the front door and as Hobson took Raindrop's head, Charles alighted.

He walked up the steps.

The front door was open, but there appeared to be no one inside.

There was no knocker on the door and he therefore knocked as loudly as he could with his closed fist.

After a few seconds there was still no response.

He was just wondering if he should knock again or go in when a girl appeared.

At first glance Charles was surprised how attractive she was.

In fact her face was more than pretty, it was lovely.

Then he noticed that her clothes were out-of-date and somewhat shabby.

She looked surprised, Charles thought, both at him and the phaeton behind him.

"I am so sorry to bother you," he began, "but one of my horses has cast a shoe and we were told in the village that you have a forge."

The girl smiled.

"Yes, of course, and our old groom, who will be in the stables, will show you how to work it. Will you follow me."

She walked past him down the steps with Charles following her.

As they passed the horses, he told Hobson to follow them.

"I can see that your horses are exceptional," the girl said. "I only hope we have a shoe of the right size."

"I am hoping so too."

"You must be very proud of your horses," the girl continued.

"Today when I brought them down from London, I am sure they set a new record, but I shall certainly have to be more careful on my way back."

"Yes, of course you will. Do you enjoy driving that high phaeton? I have never seen such a high one before."

"It is something new," explained Charles, "and has become the rage in London."

"It is certainly unusual, but very smart."

They had reached the stables and a very old groom came out of one of the doors.

"This gentleman's horse, Ben, has lost a shoe," said the girl, "and I hope we shall be able to find one to fit it."

"I'll 'ave a look, Miss Rania, but as you know us be short of shoes like everythin' else."

The girl did not reply to the groom, but there was a look of anxiety on her face.

It told Charles things were obviously very difficult for her here.

Hobson led the horses into the stable yard and they all inspected Raindrop's foot.

"I thinks us've somethin' as'll do," said Ben.

The girl turned to Charles.

"If you would not mind leaving your horses," she suggested, "perhaps you would like a cup of tea. You are going back to London and it is quite a long way."

"You are quite right and I would indeed enjoy a cup of tea, if it is no trouble."

"Come with me into the house."

As they did so, Charles said,

"I heard your groom call you 'Miss Rania'. That is an unusual name."

The girl chuckled.

"Everyone always makes the same comment. My name has the ancient meaning 'of Royalty', which as you can see, is something we are not indulging in at present!"

She made a gesture with her hands.

Charles was aware that the garden in the front of the house was unkempt and full of weeds. Brambles were sprouting from the bushes onto all the flowerbeds.

He did not say anything and as they walked into the house, he realised that too was in very much the same state.

Paper was peeling from the walls and the carpets were threadbare.

There were several pictures hanging in the passage, but they all needed a good cleaning and Charles thought some of them seemed antique and of value.

Rania opened the door into what was the drawing room and here again all the furniture needed much attention.

"If you wait here I will fetch the tea," said Rania.

He heard her running down the passage and he then guessed there were few if any servants in the house.

He was well aware that the drawing room had once been extremely attractive.

'I expect,' he mused, 'that it is the war which has caused all this dilapidation. They must be very hard-up to let it fall into such a state.'

Some time passed before Rania came back carrying a tray.

On it was a silver teapot, milk jug and two china cups. There was also a plate with a few sandwiches.

She put the tray down on a table near one of the sofas and poured out the tea.

"I am sorry to put you to so much trouble," Charles said apologetically.

"It is no trouble. Except that our cook is too old to come out of the kitchen. Her husband, who is the butler, has gone to the woods to see if we have snared any rabbits. If not, we shall go hungry for supper tonight."

Charles sat down.

"Is it really as bad as that?" he

enquired.

"Worse!" responded Rania.

"Surely you do not live here alone?"

Rania shook her head.

"No, of course not. My brother is with me now the war is over."

"What is he doing at the moment?"

To his surprise Rania's eyes, which were very large and blue, filled with tears.

"He is riding — Dragonfly — for the last time!"

The tears overflowed and ran down her cheeks.

She put a handkerchief up to her eyes.

"I am so sorry," she sighed. "It is foolish of me to behave like this."

She looked very small and pathetic.

Charles moved from his chair and sat down beside her on the sofa.

"Now tell me just what this is all about. It always upsets me to see a pretty woman in tears."

"You are not supposed — to see them."

"Then I will not look, but tell me why your brother is riding Dragon-fly for the last time."

"Be-cause," Rania wept in a jerky voice she could not control, "he and the only other — horse we own are to be sold tomorrow!"

"Why?"

Rania made a little gesture with her hands.

"You can see the plight we are in.

It is a question at the moment of — selling the horses or starving. Our two servants have had no wages — for the last three months."

Her voice broke again.

She rubbed her eyes fiercely, as if she resented her own weakness.

"I suppose it is the war which has brought you to this," said Charles gently, "and I expect your brother was a soldier. You have not told me his name."

"Yes, he was a soldier and after all his bravery — he has come back to *this.*"

She drew in her breath and then she told him,

"His name is Temple. Sir Harold Temple."

Charles gave an exclamation.

PALM BEACH COUNTY
LIBRARY SYSTEM

Library name: BKSBYMAIL

Date charged: 4/25/2018,
11:25
Title: Bachelor unforgiving
[large print]
Author: Jackson, Brenda
(Brenda Streater),
Call number: LP FIC
JACKSON
Item ID: R0092575075
Date due: 5/23/2018,23:59

Date charged: 4/25/2018,
11:25
Title: The Earl's revenge
[large print]
Author: Cartland, Barbara,
1902-2000,
Call number: LP FIC
CARTLAND
Item ID: R0092830298
Date due: 5/23/2018,23:59

Total checkouts for session:
2
Total checkouts:7

Check your account at:
http://www.pbclibrary.org

RESERVE REQUEST   TODAY'S DATE _____

#1   TITLE: _____
      AUTHOR: _____

#2   TITLE: _____
      AUTHOR: _____

#3   TITLE: _____
      AUTHOR: _____

                    CIRCLE ONE

WILL YOU ACCEPT A SUBSTITUTE?   YES   NO   ___ BY AUTHOR
                                                ___ BY SUBJECT

NAME: _____   PHONE: _____

STREET ADDRESS: _____

CITY: _____   ZIP CODE: _____

"Harold Temple! Of course I know him. We were at Eton together and in the same House."

"You were?" cried Rania looking at him in surprise.

"Harry was indeed a great friend of mine. He and I not only competed for Head of House, but we were both in the cricket First Eleven."

"I am sure Harry will be thrilled to see you again, but he is terribly upset, as you can imagine, to have come home to find everything in this dreadful mess."

Rania stifled a little sob and went on,

"We can no longer afford to employ anyone on the estate and the farmers, when they had eaten all their own animals, had to go to work for other people who could pay them."

Charles reflected that this story was not unique.

The war had been devastating for a great number of people in the English countryside and last year the harvest had been very bad.

It had finally ruined a great number of farmers who were trying to keep their heads above water.

What was more, the British Government was now importing cheap food from the Continent and that meant what crops the farmers were able to take to market were often unsellable.

Charles could see that talking about it upset Rania, so he said quietly,

"Today is obviously a bad day for both of us. I for myself am wondering whether I should go back to London or hide myself in the country."

Rania wiped her eyes.

"Tell me why," she enquired.

"I supposed we all have our ups and downs," he replied, "but mine has been a big shock to me."

"Tell me about it," Rania repeated.

Because he felt that his own problems might divert her from feeling so distressed, Charles continued,

"I have just proposed to a girl I thought was in love with me. But she has told me she has already accepted a man, who I think is most unpleasant, and just because he is going to be a Duke."

"How ghastly for you!" exclaimed Rania.

"I rather feel as if someone has given me a knockout blow!"

"That is not surprising. At the same time it is lucky that you had not married her. If then you discovered that she only really cared for someone else's title, there would be nothing you could do."

"That is what I am trying to tell myself."

There was a silence for a moment.

"What I am wondering about is whether I should now travel back to London to face the music with all my friends commiserating with my plight, while laughing at me behind their hands!"

He paused before adding,

"Or perhaps I should hide my head in the bushes and hope that no one will notice!"

"I do see it is quite a problem," said Rania. "But of course the right thing to do is to be brave. If people laugh at you, laugh too. But I know it will not be easy."

"To tell the truth, it will be extremely difficult and most unpleasant. When the lady in question does go ahead and announces her engagement, I shall undoubtedly look a complete fool."

Rania gave a sigh.

"I am very sorry for you, but it occurs to me that, if it was at all possible, the best way you could save yourself would be announce your own engagement first!"

Charles stared at her.

"That is an interesting idea, but the difficulty is, to whom?"

Rania smiled at him.

"Seeing your smart horses and your phaeton I am certain that a good number of girls would be only too glad to marry you and would also love you for yourself."

"I am beginning to doubt that completely. In fact, I know how the women I meet in London will only say 'yes' to the highest title available. I myself am teased by being called *'the never never Peer'.*"

"Why do they say that?"

"Because I am the heir presumptive to my uncle, who is an Earl. I expect your brother will remember him, and as he is sixty-five, he is not thinking of dying."

"You could hardly expect your poor uncle to die," laughed Rania, "just because you want to get married."

"No, of course not. I was only joking."

"At the same time it would be a splendid idea for you to announce your engagement first. Could you do it with someone who would allow you to break it off in two or three month's time? Then the girl who has treated you so badly will receive her just desserts."

Charles was thinking aloud.

"You mean if I can announce my

engagement first, everyone will think she has accepted the Duke's son purely because she has lost me."

"Exactly. There must be someone who will be able to help you. A cousin or a close friend? It will have to be someone you can trust. It would be too good a story if they told anyone what you were doing."

"You are so right, Rania, but equally I cannot think of a single woman I could ever trust. Not in London at any rate. They all gossip and go on gossiping until everyone's reputation is in shreds!"

"I have heard about that, but as I have never been to London, I am not a very good judge."

"I suppose I could pay for someone to act the part," he wondered slowly.

He was now thinking of the exceedingly attractive young women he had seen performing at Drury Lane.

Then he remembered that his relations would have to believe his engagement was a genuine one as they would be horrified at the thought of him marrying an actress.

He made an empty gesture with his hands.

"I think, although it is a clever idea of yours, it is really impossible."

"I am sorry," said Rania in a soft voice. "I do wish I could help you. We are both in the same boat. Fate is too strong for us and this is a battle neither of us can win."

Charles suddenly stared at her.

"What is it?" she asked. "What are you thinking?"

"I have suddenly thought of something."

"What is it?"

"If I was to offer you one thousand pounds, would you pretend to be my fiancée?"

CHAPTER TWO

Rania turned her head away.

"I don't think that is very funny," she said sternly.

"It's not a joke," replied Charles. "I mean it!"

She turned back to look at him and he could see the astonishment in her eyes.

"Are — you really — suggesting —" she stammered.

"Now listen, Rania, if I give you a thousand pounds you can keep your horses and you can do a great deal that I see needs doing in this house. I will be frank and say that I can well afford it. At the same time you will be doing me a really good turn."

She made a helpless gesture with her hands.

"But it — is impossible. It would be wonderful for us — of course it would. But how would anyone — believe that you wanted — to marry *me*?"

Charles smiled.

"You are most beautiful and if you were properly dressed you would be a sensation in the *Beau Monde.*"

"Are you seriously suggesting that the people you know and who you want to impress would accept me?"

"You are your father's daughter," replied Charles, "and he was always respected. You are feeling miserable because at the moment owing to the war, you are hard-up. I am quite certain that if Harry has one thousand pounds to start with, he can do a great deal not only in the house but on the estate."

"Of course he could," she agreed. "But I am sure he would object very strongly — that I should act a lie."

"The first and most important consideration is that he should not know."

Rania drew in her breath.

"You mean that we should not — tell him the truth?"

"Of course not. If you are doing

anything secretive, it is so essential that no one, and I mean no one, should be aware of what is happening."

He was thinking of some of the dangerous missions he had undertaken in the war that had been very successful, because he was so strict on preserving secrecy.

"But you can trust — my brother."

"If we are doing something like this, we trust no one. The only people who must know what is happening are you and me."

"Do you — really think we can — get away with it?"

She thought as she spoke how wonderful it would be to have one thousand pounds to spend.

It would save Dragonfly from having to be sold and perhaps they would be able to buy some new horses for the stables.

They could also afford to pay the wages of Johnson and his wife and Mrs. Johnson could take on extra help in the kitchen.

They could actually re-engage the housemaids who they had to send away and there would be help for poor old Ben in the stables.

Charles was watching her face and he knew exactly what she was thinking.

"You could do all that," he told her quietly, "and a great deal more. I will buy you the clothes you will need to wear in London."

For a moment Rania's expressive

eyes lit up.

"My Mama would be very shocked at my accepting anything — so expensive from a gentleman."

"I cannot believe that your mother would want you to look as you look now and continue to eat nothing but rabbits!"

Rania walked to the window and looked out at the garden. It had once been neat, tidy and filled with flowers, but now there were more weeds than flowers.

She knew it would break her mother's heart to see what a sorry state it was in.

Charles did not speak as he was wise in his dealings with other people and knew it was important to give them time to decide whether or not to do what he wanted.

Rania turned round.

"Harry will be home soon. Will he really — believe that you appeared out of nowhere just to ask me — to marry you?"

"Leave it to me," said Charles confidently. "I can be very convincing when something important is at stake. As far I am concerned this is the most important issue to happen to me since the Battle of Waterloo!"

Rania smiled as he had meant her to.

"You cannot compare the two."

"I can. At the Battle of Waterloo I was attempting to save my life, now I am trying to save my reputation!"

Rania did not speak and he continued,

"I will plead with you on my knees if necessary to help me. I know exactly how much they will laugh at me when they find out that Shaw, an unpopular and unpleasant little man, has defeated me almost at the altar steps."

There was no doubt from the way he spoke that it meant a great deal to him.

"If you are quite — quite certain that I will not make things worse — and you will not be angry with me if I make mistakes — then I will do it."

"Thank you so very much. I am more grateful than I can possibly put into words. Now I want you to wear this — in order to convince your brother that I am serious."

He brought out of his pocket the velvet box which contained Silver's engagement ring.

Next he opened the box and held it out to Rania and she drew in her breath.

"It is beautiful! The most beautiful ring I have ever seen!"

"Let me put it on for you, Rania."

He took her left hand and slipped the ring onto her third finger.

It fitted without difficulty.

"I will be very, very careful with it and I will give it back as soon as our pretend engagement comes to an end."

"It certainly becomes you and with your beauty you will find a great many men in the future will want to give you diamonds."

Rania laughed.

"I think that is most unlikely, but if we are able to keep Dragonfly I will not ask for anything more."

Charles thought her words were very touching.

She obviously knew very little of the world outside this dilapidated house and its neglected estate.

Her beauty, once it was properly framed, would not go unnoticed in London.

Perhaps when the appropriate time came to end the engagement, it would be reasonably easy and she would have fallen in love with someone who really loved her.

Aloud he said,

"Now before Harry returns, you

must promise me once again that you will not let anyone else know of our arrangement and that you will appear to be as enamoured with me as I am with you."

"I will try, I promise you I will really try. But I am afraid that Harry will think it most strange that I have not mentioned you to him before."

"Leave that problem to me," Charles assured her.

Even as he spoke they heard steps coming down the corridor.

A second later Sir Harold Temple opened the door and walked in.

"I am back, Rania," he called.

Then he saw Charles.

"Good Heavens, Charles!" he exclaimed loudly in surprise.

"Where on earth have you sprung from?"

"I am so delighted to see you, Harry. I would have been here before, but I have been in the North of England."

"Well, I am delighted that you are here now. I have often thought of the fun we had at Eton, especially when you made fifty in the match against Harrow."

Charles laughed.

"Fancy you remembering that! I was very proud of myself at the time."

"And we were all very proud of you, Charles."

Harry looked towards Rania.

"I expect you remember Rania. But she must have grown a great deal since you last saw her."

"Actually, Harry," Charles now ventured. "She is the reason for my visit. It may surprise you, but Rania has done me the great honour of promising to be my wife!"

Harry stared at him as if he could not believe his ears.

Rania thought she must do something, so she went up to Harry and slipped her arm through his.

"It is true, Harry, and I am very, very happy."

"But, Rania, you have never mentioned Charles to me," exclaimed Harry in a bewildered voice. "You never even told me you had seen him since we were children."

"I am afraid it is my fault," Charles broke in before Rania

could speak. "When I came back from the Army of Occupation, I spent a little time in London and then had to go up to Northumberland to see my uncle."

Harry nodded to show he knew who he meant and Charles went on,

"I had written frequently to Rania whenever I could throughout the war, but most of my letters never arrived and very foolishly she thought I had forgotten her."

He smiled at Rania before he added,

"She has forgiven me and if you will look at her left hand you will see that we are formally engaged."

Rania held out her left hand and Harry looked at the ring in astonishment.

For a moment he did not speak.

Rania guessed he was calculating how much it must have cost.

"Where have you left Dragonfly?" she asked Harry.

"I put him in the paddock. It saved me going to the stables and I thought you would want to put him to bed."

He nearly added — *'for the last time.'*

Then he became afraid of the unhappy and stricken expression that would appear in his sister's eyes.

"I will go and talk to him, Harry. Will you please entertain our visitor?"

"That is a good idea," Charles

came in, "as I have several things to say to Harry. But don't be too long. You know we have to make plans to go to London tomorrow."

"To London!" Harry exclaimed before Rania could do the same.

She stopped herself from repeating the words and slipped out of the room.

Outside she listened for a moment and heard Harry saying,

"I must admit that this has taken me completely by surprise. I do not know if I am on my head or my heels!"

"I realise, Harry, that you have been though a rather difficult time. Therefore I am not only going to marry your sister, but first thing on Monday morning I am going to tell my bank to transfer one thousand pounds into yours. More important than anything else, you will not have to sell your horses."

"But you cannot do that," answered Harry quickly.

"I can and I will. After all we have been friends since we were boys and if I was in the same predicament I would turn to you for help and I do not believe you would say 'no!' "

"Of course I wouldn't if I could, Charles, but how can I accept your money? There is no chance whatever of my being able to pay it back."

"I do not want it back. As you must know, I am a very rich man, and as I was spending very little during the war it has accumulated until I am rather ashamed of having so much when many of my friends have little or nothing."

"That is truly me."

"I do know. Rania told me what you are up against and I am not only exceedingly sorry for you, but I also need your help."

"My help?"

Rania was still listening outside the door.

She wondered if, after all that Charles had said, he was now going to tell Harry the truth about their pretended engagement.

"You came back from the war to find things in a terrible mess," Charles began. "I also have found there is a great deal to be done at

Lyndon Hall."

"I can hardly believe that," replied Harry. "I have always thought of it as the most perfect house I have ever seen. In fact it is really only fit for a King!"

Charles chortled.

"I have not yet been crowned and there are a good number of changes I want to undertake before I feel I am 'Monarch of all I survey'. That is where *you* come in."

"In what way?" enquired Harry.

"Firstly, I want your help and advice on planning a private Race-course. It is something I have always thought was missing at Lyndon Hall. Now I intend with your help to build one immediately."

"With my help?" murmured

Harry.

"You and I have always enjoyed life in the same way," replied Charles, "and I want you to spend as much time as you can spare for the planning of my Racecourse and supervising it when I am not there."

He gave a little laugh.

"You have not asked the obvious question — 'where are the racehorses?'"

"You owned some before the war," said Harry, "or rather your father did. I remember he won the Gold Cup at Ascot."

"Which I certainly intend to do again, but as you can imagine, the horses my father bred have grown old and those that died or were put out to grass have never been replaced. That, once again, is where you come in."

"Do you really mean it, Charles?"

"I know no one else who is a better judge of a horse than you, and as I have just said we always like the same things, but if I am taking Rania to meet all my relatives, I cannot be attending at Tattersall's sale rooms and looking round the countryside for the sort of horse that you and I know instinctively is a winner."

Harry put his hand up to his forehead.

"I just cannot believe that this is really happening. I have been in such a dreadful state of despair that I almost wished one of those French bullets had hit me in the heart rather than in the leg!"

"I was told that was why you could not take part in the Army of Occupation."

"I was laid up for some time, firstly in France and then I could not do much when I returned to England. But now I am as fit as a fiddle!"

Charles chuckled.

"I remember you saying that at Eton and boasting about your progress in the gymnasium."

"Well if you really mean me to do these things for you —"

Rania moved away from outside the door.

She had heard the most important parts and Charles had been most astute in diverting Harry's attention from their engagement.

He would now be thinking and dreaming of horses, so he would not ask the awkward questions she had feared.

She ran out to the paddock and Dragonfly, realising that she was there, came galloping towards her and started nuzzling against her.

Finally she took him back into the stables, where she could see the Highflyer phaeton and the horses which had drawn it.

"That be the strangest carriage I've ever seen, Miss Rania," grunted Ben.

"I agree with you it is very odd looking, but, Ben, I expect is goes very fast."

"Too fast for I, miss, I'd be feared

for me life 'igh up in the air."

"I promise you, Ben, that Sir Harold will not ask you to drive one!"

She went inside the stables to admire the perfectly matched team.

The horse which had lost its shoe now had a new one.

She was informed that Charles's groom was having something to eat in the kitchen.

When she had finished inspecting Charles's horses, she walked slowly back into the house.

The two men were still talking and as she entered the drawing room she knew by the expression on Charles's face that all was well.

"I have been admiring your horses," she told him. "I have never seen such a perfectly matched team."

"I thought they might please you," replied Charles. "I have now arranged with Harry that I will drive you to London, not in my Highflyer, which as you know has only room for a driver, but in your carriage which can be drawn by your horses."

"Is Harry coming with us?"

"No, I have persuaded him to slip over to Lyndon Hall in my High-flyer as he has something to inspect there before he joins us."

Rania remembered she was not supposed to know about the Race-course, so she said nothing.

"I am afraid that you will find our phaeton old and creaky," volunteered Harry.

"But no one can dispute that the horses are not first-class," Rania added hastily, "and I shall be most hurt if C-Charles does not admire them."

She stumbled a little over his Christian name, but Harry did not seem to notice and she guessed that he was thinking with unconcealed delight that he was now to drive the Highflyer.

They had talked about these new phaetons before and she knew it would please him enormously to drive one.

It was exceedingly kind and clever of Charles to have thought of his doing so.

"Charles will be staying the

night," Harry told her a little belatedly, "so I hope you will make him comfortable. I am going down to the cellar to see if there is anything left to drink."

"I shall be surprised if there is," replied Rania. "I thought you brought up the last bottle a month or so ago."

"Don't worry about that," said Charles. "It is more important to eat than drink. Rania and I will have plenty of that later when everyone will want to drink our health."

"I hope not too many people too quickly —" sighed Rania nervously.

"I am afraid it is something we shall not be able to avoid. My family will undoubtedly want to celebrate that the perennial bachelor has been caught at last!"

They all laughed.

"I only wish your mother was alive," said Rania. "I remember her coming here once when I was very small. I sat on her knee and she told me a story about fairies that hovered over the flowers and looked more like butterflies. I have been looking for them ever since!"

"I did not realise you knew my mother."

"You were at Eton at the time with Harry. I think your father and mother had come to visit you and stopped on their way back to tell my parents that Harry was in good health and they were not to worry about him."

"It was so like my mother to think of that."

Rania realised by the way he spoke that his mother had meant a great deal to him and she thought perhaps she would be pleased now that she was helping to prevent him from being laughed at.

She would have been so horrified that he had been jilted by an unkind and cruel beauty.

Rania jumped up from her chair.

"If you are staying for dinner, I will have to go and see if there is anything to eat. But I am afraid it is likely to be rabbit."

She left the room and Harry commented,

"Rania has been absolutely wonderful. Not only by staying here alone when our parents died, but also by never complaining about the terrible predicament we are in."

He paused for a moment.

"I was only thinking today when I was riding that it would break her heart when we sold Dragonfly to-morrow."

"I will promise you faithfully, Harry, that she shall have the best horses it is possible to buy and I will arrange for her, when we are staying in London, to ride with me every morning in Rotten Row."

"I cannot imagine anyone that I would rather Rania marry than you," Harry now blurted out.

He gave a little laugh before he added,

"It never crossed my mind, however, that anything so marvellous was even a possibility."

"I promise you I will look after her and try to make her happy."

"Well, the first thing she must have is some clothes. Because times have been so bad, I don't think that she has bought any thing for herself for the last two or three years."

"I will see to it. So do not worry."

"I feel so embarrassed at taking so much from you, Charles," protested Harry.

"As I have already indicated, there is no need for anything to be embarrassing or uncomfortable between us. If our positions were reversed you would help me and I am certainly not going to be a Pharisee and pass you by on the other side."

Harry laughed.

"I could never see you passing by, Charles. You have always been exceedingly kind to just about everyone. I do remember you comforting all the small boys at Eton when they were homesick or when they had been beaten by the prefects."

Charles sighed.

"That seems a long time ago and sometimes I think I was happier then than at any other time in my life."

"Nonsense," Harry protested again. "I know what a success you were in the war and if we cannot cope with the peace we should be ashamed of ourselves. But I admit that was how I was feeling until you turned up today."

"Put your own house in order," Charles urged him, "and do not spare the expense. Then help me with mine."

Rania found Mrs. Johnson almost in tears.

"Now whatever can I give a smart gentleman to eat, Miss Rania?" she asked. "There's nothin' in the house and all I has for you and the Master this evening is a bit of old rabbit left over from yesterday."

"He certainly will not thrive on that," sighed Rania.

She turned to walk back the way she had come and as she did so she saw Charles's groom.

He was sitting in what had once

been the servants' hall reading a newspaper, which she reckoned must have been days or perhaps weeks old and yet he was reading it because he had nothing else to do.

She ran quickly back to the drawing room.

The two men were laughing as she went in.

"I am sorry to disturb you," she began, "but there is nothing for dinner unless your groom can run down to the village and buy something from the butcher."

She spoke with a slight note of aggression in her voice and it was almost as if she was challenging Charles.

"His name is Watson. Tell him to buy everything you require not only for tonight and tomorrow's break-fast, but for the rest of the staff for a week or so. I doubt if we will be able to come back as quickly as we would like to."

As Charles spoke he took a note of the value of ten pounds from his pocket and handed it to Rania.

"That is — too much!" she ex-claimed.

"I was just thinking it is far too little for what we require. Let me arrange matters with Harry and you take this to Watson."

Rania took the note.

Then because she felt too embar-rassed to say any more, she ran from the room.

Charles next pulled another four notes of the same denomination out of his pocket.

"You will need cash, Harry, for yourself tomorrow and for the servants who will look after your house while you are looking after mine."

"It's no use me protesting. You know only too well what I am feeling, but frankly, Charles, there is nothing I can do except to thank you profusely."

"I do not want to be thanked, because I am taking from you something that is far more valuable, which is, as you know, your sister."

He slapped his shoulder and cried,

"For goodness sake, Harry, do stop worrying about money. We shared what pocket-money we had when we were at Eton and as far as I am concerned we share what either of us has at the moment. Personally I think I have the best deal."

Harry realised he was referring to Rania.

"There I do agree with you. She is an exceptional person and very intelligent, just as my mother was. They adore her in the village even though we cannot do anything financially to help them. That, incidentally, is where the money you are giving me will go to in the first place."

"I thought you would say just that and please don't worry about how you spend it. There is plenty more, thank God, where those notes come from."

Back in the kitchen Rania was making a quick note of everything Mrs. Johnson required including a bottle of wine, as she was quite certain Johnson would find nothing in the cellar.

"I don't suppose they will have champagne in the village, but it would be most appropriate to celebrate my engagement to Captain Lyndon."

"Your engagement!" exclaimed Mrs. Johnson. "But why didn't you tell us before? It's the most excitin' news I've heard since the war were over."

Rania showed off her ring and Mrs. Johnson was suitably impressed.

Finally Watson was sent off to the village with the ten pound note and a long list of what was required.

"I knew as 'ow things would definitely change for the better," Mrs. Johnson said finally. "Us couldn't go on as us were as I says to God in me prayers, what'll become of us when there's not a penny left? This be His answer."

"You have been so wonderful to us through all our troubles," said Rania. "Sir Harry will give you your wages tomorrow and all we owe you for the last three months."

She kissed the old woman before she added,

"We never rewarded you and Johnson for being so kind and never making a fuss when things got worse and — *worse.*"

Her voice broke on the last word.

"Now don't you go upsettin' yourself, miss. You have a good man who'll make you 'appy and that's all I've ever wanted for you."

"We are very lucky," she sighed, wiping her eyes.

Mrs. Johnson sat down on her chair.

"Over and over again," she said, "Mr. Johnson says to me, 'us can't go on like this,' and I says to 'im I says, 'God'll help us sooner or later!' "

Rania could not help thinking it was wrong of her to deceive these dear people as they had been so wonderful through all their difficulties.

She wished it was the truth and that she was really getting married and if it was to someone rich like Charles Lyndon they would never want again.

Then she told herself she was being greedy.

He was really just like an Archangel coming down from Heaven.

He had appeared when she was desperate at losing Dragonfly and Harry was in the depths of despair.

What she was doing for Charles would save them all and she was sure that while they were busy spending the fabulous one thousand pounds he had promised for them, something new would turn up.

Harry would find a good way of

making money so that they would not starve again.

'We have been so incredibly lucky,' Rania told herself.

That night at dinner she thought that it would have been impossible for three people to laugh more or for them to enjoy themselves as much as did.

A bottle of champagne had been procured and Mrs. Johnson excelled herself.

There was fresh fish from the river, good roast beef and a delicious pudding.

Rania was thinking that it might seem just a simple meal to Charles, but for Harry and herself it was ambrosia, a gift from the Gods.

She managed to find an evening

dress she had not worn for years, which had belonged to her mother and had been altered for her. It was very simple and yet elegant.

She took a great deal of trouble with her hair.

Charles seemed to be stunned by her beauty when she came into the drawing room.

She had looked lovely in the shabby dress she had been wearing in the daytime, but now he knew she would grace any London ball-room.

It would have been impossible for any man present not to look at her and look again.

Charles had brought his evening clothes with him, as he had thought it very likely that Silver would ask him to stay the night.

He looked overwhelmingly hand-some, Rania now decided.

In her vivid imagination she saw the medals he had received on the battlefields glinting away on his cut-away evening coat.

Harry's evening clothes were not so smart and were somewhat out-of-date, but at least he was the same height as Charles.

Taken together it would have been impossible for any woman not to think they were a pair of ex-tremely good looking and attractive young men.

Johnson had done his best to make the dining table look festive for such a special occasion and he had brought the silver candlesticks out of the safe.

While Rania and Harry were dining alone they had told him not to bother, as it would have given him so much extra work and there was so little to eat anyway they were only in the dining room for a few minutes.

Now with flowers hurriedly picked from the garden in the centre of the table and all the candles lit, it all looked very glamorous to Rania.

'It is all due to Charles,' she mused. 'I shall never be grateful enough to him for his turning up at the very last moment before I lost Dragonfly!'

Harry lifted up the last glass of champagne for the bottle was now empty.

"I am now going to drink to the health of the engaged couple," he announced, "and hope that this is the first day of a long life of happiness together."

He paused to smile at them before he continued,

"You are the two people I love best in the world, and for me nothing could be more marvellous than that you should be together. God bless you both and may you never lose the love and happiness you have now."

He spoke with such deep and sincere emotion that Rania felt tears come into her eyes.

But she was ashamed that they were deceiving him.

She looked across the table at Charles and knew he understood her thoughts.

"Thank you very much, Harry," he said, "and now that I am leg-shackled by Rania, I will set out to find you a charming wife so that you will feel just as happy as we are tonight."

Harry laughed.

Rania felt Charles had cleverly turned a sentimental moment into an amusing one.

"Now you are frightening me," protested Harry. "I have no wish to be married and, as you can see, I have at the moment nothing to offer a bride but a dilapidated house and empty fields."

"That is going to change," insisted

Charles. "Good luck is with us and just as I have it now, so will you. We have always done everything together and fate will not let us down in the future."

"I hope you are right," replied Harry, "and I have never felt as happy as I do at this moment."

"And of course I can say the same."

Rania felt that she ought to say something.

But somehow the words stuck in her throat.

They were deceiving Harry in the same way as they were deceiving Johnson and Mrs. Johnson.

And tomorrow they would be deceiving Charles's relations.

'It is — wrong! It is — wrong!'

she cried in her heart.

Equally she could not help feeling overwhelmingly grateful — they had been rescued from the very depths of depression.

Now the only question was what lay ahead when all these lies and deception were no longer necessary and her pretend engagement to Charles came to an end.

CHAPTER THREE

Driving away from their house Rania felt that she was setting off on an adventure.

It was the most exciting thing to have happened to her in her entire life.

Charles had insisted on Harry driving off first as he wanted to make sure his horses were in perfect condition especially after his own horse had been shoed.

Actually, Rania thought, he really wanted to be sure that Harry could handle the Highflyer phaeton.

But Harry was such an experienced driver she was certain he could handle anything and he drove it with the same expertise that Charles had shown.

They watched him go down the drive and Charles gave a little sigh of relief when he disappeared out of sight.

"Now we must be off, Rania. I have given Harry enough money not only for the journey to my house but also for the servants. Just so that you will not worry while we are staying in London, I am giving them enough to feed themselves for a month."

Rania put her hand on his arm.

"How can you be so kind? Harry

is embarrassed, as he told me this morning, at taking so much from you, but he will work his fingers to the bone because he is just so grateful."

Charles smiled at her.

"And so you must make yourself the most beautiful lady London has ever seen. That will be a slap in the eye for those who might think I have lost Silver!"

He said her name and then wished he had not.

He was quite sure anyway that his relations would undoubtedly tell Rania that they were so surprised at their sudden engagement, as they had been sure he was going to marry the ravishing Silver Bancroft.

Rania had a great deal of trouble

in finding herself something to wear as the few clothes she owned were all ragged and faded with washing.

She had not bought a new dress for years, but then she remembered all her mother's clothes, which were still hanging up in the wardrobe in her bedroom which no one had used since she died.

She ran upstairs to take a look.

She found what she thought was an attractive blue travelling gown with a cape to wear over the shoulders.

She could well remember her mother wearing it at the races and she had also worn it to a luncheon party in the neighbourhood.

And there was a pretty little bonnet trimmed with blue flowers which went with it.

Rania had not had any chance to see the fashions in the ladies' magazines nor had she seen any other pictures, which appeared from time to time, of fashionable clothes.

But occasionally someone in the village, usually the Vicar's wife, bought a fashion magazine and when she had finished with it she used to pass it on to Rania.

She therefore did not realise that since the war had ended clothes had become more elaborate and flowing than they were previously.

Her mother's clothes had all been bought before the war started and as Rania looked at the bonnet, she thought it looked rather bare.

People in London would know at once that she was no more than just a country maid so she took some feathers from another hat to add to the bonnet.

Actually, framing her small pointed face, the effect was very becoming.

When they were well away from the house, Charles said,

"Now the first thing when we arrive in London is to keep you completely hidden until I have made you look very beautiful."

"I only hope you are not boasting, Charles."

"You will be most surprised what clothes can do for a woman. You will have to stay inside my house and I am telling no one that you are there."

His voice rose as he went on,

"Tomorrow the best London dressmakers will come flooding in to show you the most fabulous and glamorous garments they possess."

"It sounds very exciting," Rania admitted in a small voice. "At the same time if when they have done their best you are disappointed, you must not be angry with me."

"I think you will be surprised at how amazing you will look. Then we will sweep out to stun the world with my engagement and your beauty!"

The way he said it made Rania laugh and then she murmured,

"I can only hope they are stunned. It will be very humiliating if they pay no attention to me!"

Charles was ruminating that it was essential for his engagement to be announced in the newspapers as quickly as possible.

He was determined to send Major Monsell to *The Gazette* and all the other newspapers as soon as he could and he was now working out in his mind exactly how the announcement should be worded.

He was afraid that by some piece of bad luck Silver would get her engagement to Wilfred Shaw in first.

But that was unlikely, he thought, unless they were rushing to publish it before the Duke actually died.

There were still far too many snags in the way of his achieving exactly what he wanted and yet he knew that what now really mattered was to reach London as quickly as possible and then he could start the wheels moving in the direction he desired.

He therefore concentrated on his driving and said very little.

Rania was happy looking at the countryside whilst thinking about how well Dragonfly and Jackal were pulling their old travelling chariot.

It had not been used for years and yet Charles had chosen it because he wanted the lightest of the carriages in the coach house.

He hoped that no one would notice them and so it really did not matter what the vehicle looked like as long as they reached their destination.

On the whole everything was going more smoothly than he had hoped and he knew that the revelation that he was engaged was going to be a shock, but a delightful one, for his relatives.

Yet he did not need for them to ask him too many questions, especially if it involved Rania in too many more lies.

He was well aware that she was distressed by the lie she was acting, but equally she was extremely grateful to him for helping Harry and saving her beloved horses.

Actually he concluded that she was quite right to be shocked at their pretend engagement.

And because she was saving his

face and he had saved their home, even the most strait-laced critic should not complain.

They stopped once to let the horses drink and then they sped on without any refreshment for themselves.

Charles had enjoyed a good breakfast, but because Rania was still worrying over her appearance, she had only snatched a mouthful and drunk one cup of coffee.

She was, therefore, feeling decidedly hungry when the first houses appeared on the outskirts of London and it was nearly time for luncheon.

As they moved through the traffic, Charles said,

"I must commend you, Rania, for

being a very good travelling companion."

"You mean because I have not talked too much? My Papa always told me how he disliked talkative women when he was concentrating on his horses and I felt that you would be the same."

"You are quite right," he agreed, "and thank you for a comfortable and quick journey."

"You must thank Dragonfly and Jackal for that and I expect they will be as excited as I am to be in London."

"I know my Head Groom will admire them too and I promise you they will be as comfortable as you will be."

Rania smiled, but he realised

without saying so that she was beginning to become nervous.

When they turned into Berkeley Square, she could see his house on the far side and she gave a little gasp.

It was a very impressive mansion.

Lyndon Hall in the country had been altered, styled and rebuilt by Robert Adam and he had done the same to the rather ugly house the Earls of Lyndonmore had owned in Berkeley Square for several generations.

Now it had become a most beautiful building and Rania thought it was impossible for a London house to be more spectacular.

She was to discover later that there was a garden at the back of

Charles's house that connected with the garden belonging to the Duke of Devonshire which sloped down from Piccadilly.

They drew up outside Lyndon House.

Two footmen in smart livery and powdered hair ran out immediately to put down a red carpet.

Charles helped Rania to alight.

"I hope you will admire my house. I have always thought it one of the finest in London. My uncle gave it to me some years ago because he never leaves the country."

"It was certainly a handsome present, Charles, and I am sure you thanked him effusively for it."

"I assure you I am famed for my good manners," he replied jokingly.

"And you have so much to be thankful for," Rania told him seriously.

She felt overawed by the entrance hall with its fine staircase and exquisitely carved marble fireplace.

There were two more footmen and a butler bowing to them as they entered.

Charles said he wanted luncheon served as quickly as possible.

Rania thought what a commotion there would be at home if a meal was ordered suddenly without any warning, but Charles's servants seemed unperturbed.

"I will bring a bottle of champagne, sir," the butler intoned, "into the study and will inform Chef of your arrival."

Rania was taken up the stairs to the most attractive bedroom she had ever seen.

There was large four-poster bed, which was carved around the top and up the posts with birds and butterflies. They were glittering with gold leaf, but so cleverly carved that they might have been real.

She took off her cape and bonnet.

A housemaid poured out some warm water so that she could wash her face and hands.

The housekeeper was a bit over-powering with her black silk gown and silver chatelaine at her waist.

She supervised the maids and then asked Rania if she wanted

anything from her trunk that had been brought upstairs whilst she was washing her hands.

"I am afraid there is very little in it," replied Rania. "I am expecting to buy a lot of clothes tomorrow, so I have brought very little with me from the country where I have been living for a long time."

She did not feel like answering any more questions until she had asked Charles what she should say.

She therefore hurriedly went downstairs to find him in the study, which was very similar in size to the one at home and the real difference lay in that everything Charles possessed was polished and shining.

Even though his staff had not

been expecting him, there were flowers on the tables.

The sunshine coming through the window glistened on a gold inkpot and there were exquisite pieces of Sevres china on the mantelpiece.

While she was upstairs Charles had already sent for Major Monsell.

He handed him a piece of paper on which he had written out the announcement to go into the newspapers.

"I know it is Sunday, Major, but if you go to Fleet Street now you might be able to persuade them to put it in tomorrow's papers. Otherwise it will have to be Tuesday."

"I think there will be no difficulty in getting it in for tomorrow," replied Major Monsell. "Anyway I will do my best, and may I congratulate you on what I am sure will be a big surprise to your relatives and to everyone else!"

"I have known my fiancée since she was a child and her brother was my best friend while I was at Eton."

He then told Major Monsell that Harry had gone to Lyndon Hall and that he was to be sent all the money he required to spend on the horses for the racing stables.

Major Monsell was far too experienced to show his surprise and Charles knew he could trust him not to gossip about these new developments in any way.

"I have brought Miss Temple to London," he told him, "but you will understand that as she has been living in the country in very poor circumstances, I do not want her to meet my family or to be seen by anyone until she has acquired some smart clothes."

Major Monsell nodded.

"I am thinking," continued Charles, "of asking one of my relatives to come and chaperone her. Until that can be arranged I would be grateful, if anyone asks, if you will say your wife is looking after Miss Temple."

"Of course, that will be quite easy."

When Charles had first engaged the Major, he had nowhere to live and had therefore given him and his wife what was to all intents and purposes a private flat of their own in the house.

Lyndon House was huge and far too large, Charles had thought at the time for a bachelor, so he had furnished three rooms for the Monsells and added a small kitchen so that they could be completely independent of his staff.

They all seemed happy with the arrangement and it certainly made matters easier at this particular moment.

There could be no question of any impropriety in Rania living in a bachelor household while Mrs. Monsell was present.

She was a retiring woman and there was really no reason for Rania to meet her and yet it would be impossible for anyone to criticise this arrangement.

The Major knew exactly what Charles wanted.

"If there is anything at all my wife can do to help," he said, "you know she will be only too willing to do so."

"Thank you, Major, and now let me tell you what I want first thing tomorrow morning."

He handed Major Monsell a list of the best shops in Bond Street and told him what he required their *vendeuses* to bring to Lyndon House as soon as possible.

"If you tell them it is for a trousseau they will fall over themselves. But anyway I have always found them to be very obliging."

He was remembering with a faint smile how he had dressed one of his Cyprians from one of the shops and she had been thrilled with the clothes they produced for her.

She had not been able to afford so many expensive dresses until she had found a rich protector and he recalled how she had paid him for his generosity and she had been such a great success that she had been given the best parts in Drury Lane.

She had also been pursued by so many men that in the end he became bored with her.

His list of what he now required for Rania was very comprehensive.

The Major glanced at it. He knew that all the shops in question would send their *vendeuses* and perhaps even their Manageress hurrying to Lyndon House.

The Major was just about to leave the study with his instructions when Rania was shown in by the butler and he considered at first glance that Rania was surely the prettiest girl he had seen.

She also had a somewhat ethereal look about her, which one certainly could not say about any of the famous London beauties.

The Major thought she appeared a little shy when Charles introduced her and that too was something new in Lyndon House.

"Major Monsell," Charles was saying, "is not only my right hand man, but he is the real genius who keeps the whole place running so smoothly without giving me any trouble!"

"That certainly must involve magic," smiled Rania, "because I think all big houses create their own problems and unexpected catastrophes."

She was thinking of how many difficulties she had experienced at home, especially when the ceilings fell in or the chimneys became blocked.

"I can assure you," replied Charles, "that, thanks to Major Monsell, that does not happen here."

"Touch wood," added the Major firmly. "You are challenging the Powers above and although I do

not bother you, I am always prepared for the unexpected."

When the Major had hurried
away, Charles poured out a glass of
champagne for Rania.

"I wish Harry was here," she said.
"You know how much he enjoys
champagne and how seldom he
drinks it."

"I can assure you the cellar at the
Hall is packed to bursting and I am
quite certain he will not go thirsty!"

Rania was looking round the
room.

"From what I have seen of your
house so far, I am very impressed.
This is a lovely room and you must
feel happy in it."

"What we must do now, Rania, is
convince people that we are both

very happy together. As soon as you have some clothes, I am afraid we shall have to call on quite a number of my relations."

"I keep telling myself that I need not be frightened of them, because all this is only a pretend engagement, but please do not let them ask me too many questions in case I make a silly mistake."

"You are not to worry about it. All you have to do is tell them you think I am wonderful and I am quite sure they will agree with you!"

Rania laughed and it was a very pretty sound.

"Now you are being not only very conceited but, as Major Monsell said, defying fate. Please, please be careful in case this big castle of lies we are building up so cleverly falls down on our heads."

"We are far too intelligent, both of us, to allow that to happen. Now just relax, Rania, and enjoy yourself."

"I want to do so, but just give me a little time to catch my breath."

"I will give you until tomorrow afternoon," Charles asserted with a twinkle in his blue eyes.

Rania held up her hands to protest that it was not long enough when the butler announced luncheon.

They walked into the large and impressive dining room, which she reckoned could easily seat forty people.

There were fine portraits on the walls of Charles's ancestors and the decorations on the table were very pretty.

Considering the Chef had been given such short notice, luncheon was delicious.

Rania could not help thinking that if they had so much food ready for unexpected visitors, a great deal must be wasted.

Then she told herself this was not the sort of thing she had to think about when she was with Charles.

Back at home the Johnsons would now be eating heartily and counting up the back wages they had received.

She was eternally grateful to Charles.

They ate luncheon without talking a great deal and then Charles suggested to her that she should rest until it was dinner time.

"I will show you my library, where I am sure you will find some books to read. But I am afraid it is only a quarter of the size of the library at Lyndon Hall!"

"I hope Harry will tell me all about it. Like me he has found it very depressing that he could not keep up with all the interesting books which have been published lately, especially those about the war."

"I have had enough of the war without having to read about it, but Major Monsell on my instructions buys every book which is published with good reviews. I feel it is important to keep a good library up-to-date."

"Of course it is if you can afford if and I think it is very sensible of you."

Charles showed her the library and she was thrilled with it and at the same time she felt he had no wish to go on entertaining her.

She therefore chose three books she wanted to read and climbed upstairs to her bedroom to find that the maids had unpacked the small amount of clothes she had brought from home.

She put on her dressing-gown and lay down on the bed. She read two chapters of one of the books she had chosen before she fell asleep.

She had not told Charles, but she had lain awake much of last night.

Not only because she was so excited that they no longer had an empty future in front of them with no horses, but it was, although she told herself she was very stupid, because she was frightened of going to London.

Charles had been so generous and kind that she felt the only way she could repay him was by being the success he wanted her to be.

But she felt rather helpless.

She had no idea what she should say to his friends.

She had heard people gossiping in the past about the great beauties of London and they described the parties, which were given even during the war amongst those who belonged to the *Beau Monde.*

The country had been regaled by vivid accounts of the most amazing party thrown at Carlton House by the Prince Regent for the Duke of Wellington. The drink, the food, all the bands and the ornamentation in the gardens lost nothing in the telling.

'Now how could I possibly know how to behave at a party like that?' Rania asked herself.

She was not aware that once she had retired for her rest, Charles had ordered a phaeton and driven to Carlton House.

His friendship with the Prince Regent had taught him that he always liked to hear about anything unusual.

The Prince collected pictures and antiques, statues and Chinese silk for his many houses and similarly he liked to collect people who were unique in any way.

Most of all he wanted to know what was happening before anyone else was aware of it.

Charles was still hoping that his engagement would be announced in the newspapers on the next morning, but it was most important that the Prince Regent should know of it beforehand.

When he arrived at Carlton House it was to find the Prince in the Chinese room, of which he was very proud, with two or three of his friends for luncheon.

It had been a very long and drawn out meal with a succession of exotic courses and a great deal of excellent wines.

When Charles was announced, the Prince Regent jumped to his feet and held out his hand.

"I heard you were in London and I am delighted to see you, Charles."

"I have just come up from the country, Sire, and as I have something of a very personal nature to discuss with Your Royal Highness, I wonder if I could beg you to spare me a few minutes."

What he said instantly intrigued the Prince and he glanced at his guests.

The Marchioness of Hertford,

who was the Prince's chosen *bonne amie* at the moment, rose from her seat and put her hand on his arm.

"We are going into the garden," she cooed. "Join us when Mr. Lyndon has told you his secret. I only hope I shall be allowed to hear it later."

She smiled at Charles and gave him her hand.

Charles kissed it and said,

"I am sure His Royal Highness will confide in you once I have confided in him!"

The Marchioness laughed.

"I think we can be quite certain of that!"

The other guests all shook hands with Charles and when the door closed behind them, the Prince

Regent said almost as eagerly as a small boy,

"Now just what have you to tell me, Charles? I am longing to hear something new."

"This news may come as a surprise to you, Sire, but I shall be announcing my engagement tomorrow."

Some of the excitement left the Prince's eyes.

"Oh! To Silver Bancroft? That is what everyone is expecting."

"In which case, Sire, they will be disappointed!"

The Price Regent's eyes opened wide.

"You are not now marrying Silver? But everyone is quite certain that you are."

"I know it, Sire, but I am engaged to a very lovely and most attractive young lady who has not yet been seen in London."

"Someone new!" he exclaimed. "That is certainly exciting. Who is she? Tell me all about her, Charles."

He threw his questions at Charles with an eagerness which was so characteristic of the Prince Regent and which made him a marvellous host and a unique companion.

He was getting old and stout, but he still had a joy of living and so many people still found him irresistible in his old age.

He sat down rather heavily on the sofa and patted the place beside him.

"Sit down, Charles, and start at

the very beginning. Who is this beauty who no one has been allowed to see?"

"That is why I thought, Sire, that maybe you would want to see her first."

The Prince Regent was delighted.

"Of course! Of course!" he cried. "Nothing would please me more. Bring her here tomorrow. Luncheon or dinner, whichever is more convenient for you."

"I think dinner would be best, Sire, and it is most kind of Your Royal Highness."

"You have not yet told me who she is," the Prince Regent persisted.

"I expect you remember Sir Roderick Temple, who at one time commanded the Grenadiers."

The Prince Regent thought for a moment.

"Yes, yes of course. But he died, I think, a long time ago."

"Just before the war started, Sire, and his son, who inherited the Baronetcy, was my good friend at Eton. It is his sister who has promised to be my wife. They are an old and respected family and Sir Roderick was, I believe, an excellent General."

"That is good, Charles, very good!"

"I hope that was what you would say, Sire. She is amazingly beautiful and has lived in the country and never been to London in her life until now."

"If she is as beautiful as you assert, she will be a sensation! And it is high time we had some new beauties to delight us."

"I shall be interested to see if Your Royal Highness agrees with me that she is different from all the rest and is in fact, *outstanding.*"

"Good!" he exclaimed with satisfaction. "That is what we want, and if I am to introduce her to our friends, it will be an excellent excuse for me to give a party tomorrow evening."

"Not too large, Sire," said Charles hastily. "Rania is rather shy and, as I have already said, has never been to London. I do not want her scared by your magnificence."

The Prince Regent laughed.

"We will not frighten her. But if

you permit me to present her to some critical members of the *Beau Monde*, it will amuse me to see not only their astonishment, but their irritation because you have found her first!"

"I agree with you, Sire. It would be most amusing. Your Royal Highness does know just how the likes of Lord Amesworth and the Marquis of Sutherworth always think they are cleverer than anyone else at bringing you anything unusual."

The Prince Regent chuckled as he was well aware that they all wanted to maintain their position in his circle.

They were always searching for something original to intrigue and to amuse him, but they found it somewhat difficult when it came to new beauties.

Charles rose from the sofa.

"I must not keep Your Royal Highness from your guests. I can only thank you again, Sire, for your kindness in saying you will present my fiancée to the Social world."

He paused before he added,

"You know how critical they always are. But with Your Royal Highness's approval it will be very difficult for them to find too many faults!"

He knew that what he had said pleased the Prince Regent, who was rising rather slowly from the sofa.

He put his hand on Charles's shoulder and chuckled.

"It will certainly be a surprise to

them and everyone else that you are not marrying Silver Bancroft. Everyone was quite certain that she had caught you at last!"

"She certainly boasts a beautiful face, but as Your Royal Highness knows, I am very easily bored."

"That is true enough. And I shall warn this pretty creature you are bringing to me that she will have to be on her guard if she is to keep you for any length of time!"

"I do not want to prejudice Your Royal Highness's opinion, rather to let you, Sire, decide for yourself whether I am right or wrong in thinking she is unique."

"She shall have a party which will be remembered for a long time, Charles, and it will infuriate those who are not invited!"

Charles laughed.

"That is certainly true, Sire, at the same time please do not frighten her. Remember she has lived in the country in that huge house which had belonged to her father with a minimum number of servants, because of the war, with the ceilings tumbling down on her head."

"As bad as that!" exclaimed the Prince Regent.

"It is what happened to a great number of people, Sire, as you are well aware. We can only try, as Your Royal Highness has been trying, to build again what is beautiful and worthy of being preserved."

"Of course! Of course! You are right, Charles, as you always are.

We must build up England again and the ravages of war must be forgotten."

"That is just what we all hope will happen, Sire, but there is a great deal to be done, and who can tell the people what is wanted better than Your Royal Highness?"

The Prince drew in a deep breath which made him seem stouter than he was already.

"I am really doing my best, but as you well know, Charles, it is not easy."

"You have been quite magnificent, Sire, in what you have done. You have brought art, fine pictures and furniture back into fashion. You have made people aware that we have treasures in this country as yet undiscovered."

"I like to think I have done that."

"I would assure you, Sire, that you will always be remembered in the art world and I know my fiancée will be so entranced with the many treasures Your Royal Highness has collected here."

"Then she shall see them all. Seven o'clock prompt tomorrow evening and do not be late."

"We will certainly not be late, Sire. Now I must go back to my fiancée."

"May she bring you every happiness."

The Prince Regent patted Charles on the shoulder and then walked towards the door.

Charles opened it for him and

they said goodbye.

The Prince Regent went to join his friends in the garden.

Charles walked into the hall and a footman handed him his hat and cane.

As he drove away he thought that he had been very clever.

Nothing could possibly annoy Silver more than to have a new beauty take her place in the admiration of the *Beau Monde*.

If Rania was introduced and admired by the Prince Regent, the majority of the beaux and bucks would follow his lead.

As he returned to Berkeley Square he was thinking that he had struck a blow at Silver which would hurt her as much as she had hurt him.

The only vital issue he had to cope with now was to make certain that Rania would not let him down and he felt confident she would not do so.

First, as he had reflected before, her beauty must be 'framed', as at the moment it was hidden by dingy clothes and by her complete ignorance of how to make the best of her looks.

She was very lovely — a gift from God.

But it was up to mankind to see that her beauty was presented to the best advantage.

Like any dramatic heroine stepping onto a stage for the first time, she must be beautifully projected against the correct background for the audience to fully appreciate her.

He knew he had now arranged for her to appear on the finest stage possible.

Carlton House.

With that background all she required was the right gown and to have her hair arranged in the latest and most graceful fashion.

Major Monsell, Charles decided, would have to get hold of Antonio, the most popular and most sought after hairdresser in London.

He was an Italian who had introduced a number of different fashions that had become all the rage in Society and before any major ball every lady in Mayfair wanted his attention.

'He will not refuse me,' Charles

now told himself, 'especially when he knows where Rania will be dining!'

He was musing as he drove back to his house that Rania's hair was undoubtedly her crowning glory and as she was to be married to him, she could wear some of the magnificent jewels which had belonged to his mother.

But not the family tiara, as that was kept especially for married women. However, there were several diamond stars she could wear in her hair and they would match the diamonds that would encircle her long neck.

Charles was still planning all the details of Rania's first step into Society when he drew up his horses outside Lyndon House.

The red carpet was rolled out for him as usual and he walked up the steps thinking he had been very astute.

It gave him almost as much satisfaction as when in the war he had taken some of the enemy by surprise and they were either dead or taken prisoners before they could think about how to defend themselves.

Tomorrow night he would be fighting back against Silver and he was quite certain that he would be the victor before the battle even began.

CHAPTER FOUR

Charles did not send for Rania after he had arrived back home and so she did not see him until she came downstairs for dinner.

The only dress she could wear was the one she had worn the previous night with Harry.

Because it suited her so well, Charles thought she looked even lovelier than she had then.

He had eaten dinner with many women and yet he could not remember ever having one with a woman who did not talk about herself incessantly or flirt with him.

Rania plied him with plenty of questions about his house, which he was delighted to answer.

They had a few little arguments on issues of history and to his surprise Charles had to admit she was right and he was wrong.

When they both walked into the drawing room after dinner, Rania said,

"It is so exciting being able to talk to you as I have had no one to talk to as we have tonight since Papa died."

"What about Harry?" enquired Charles.

"Oh, Harry talks about horses and the estate and, of course, most of our discussions have been gloomy lately."

"Well, that is all forgotten now and after tomorrow night you will, I am quite certain, only want to talk about yourself."

Rania laughed.

"I would find it an extremely dull subject. I would much rather talk about the world and the people you have met who were specialists in whatever they did."

Charles thought this was such a different approach from anything he had been asked previously and he did his best to tell Rania about the distinguished people he had met in Paris at the time of the Occupation.

She was particularly interested in

the Ambassadors from other countries.

They had lingered over dinner longer than he had intended and when finally he glanced at the clock he was astonished to see it was already half-past eleven.

"You must go to bed at once, Rania, I want you to look your very best tomorrow night with no lines under your eyes!"

"I am not likely at my age to have lines, but if I am not wanted I will of course withdraw."

She was laughing as she spoke and added,

"You know I want to say thank you for everything you are doing for us. For all your overwhelming kindness, there are just not enough words in the English language to express what I feel."

"I do not want to be thanked, Rania, only that you will put on an act tomorrow night which will, I hope, make you shine like a star in the sky."

"I only hope I can do that without falling down and smashing at your feet. That at least would be dramatic, but not what you require!"

"Go to bed," he ordered, opening the door for her, "and remember I am the stage manager of this drama and therefore you have to obey me!"

"Naturally, sir. How could I do anything else?" she replied mockingly.

As she was speaking she dropped

him a low curtsy, then laughing ran along the passage towards the hall.

Charles thought that she was more fun than anyone he had ever met and he was making full use of her at the moment for his own ends.

Later he would do his best to find her a charming and rich husband before she had to return to the country.

He ran over the names of his friends in his mind, but he could not think of anyone particularly outstanding who deserved a wife as beautiful and amusing as Rania.

She found a maid waiting to help her to undress and climbed into her comfortable bed.

Everything, she mused, was so

exciting and Harry would no longer be worried and unhappy.

'Thank you, God, thank you,' she prayed over and over again before she fell asleep.

Charles hurried down to breakfast at eight o'clock the next morning, as he wished to see the newspapers.

He had found a note from Major Monsell last night saying,

"I did manage to place the announcement of your engagement into the Gazette and all the daily newspapers for tomorrow morning.

The editors were very interested and will be writing an editorial about you and your war record.

John Monsell."

He was delighted that the announcement would be published before the Carlton House dinner party.

Those not invited would be extremely annoyed they were not being offered the first glimpse of Rania.

Whether it was his future wife or the latest beauty was immaterial. They would undoubtedly want to see her if for nothing else because she was a new face.

He had only just finished breakfast when the first collection of clothes arrived.

In came the shop's Manageress, a *vendeuse* and two girls to carry the gowns.

Charles had already informed his

housekeeper that as Rania would be trying on clothes, she was to be served breakfast in bed.

Additionally he had decided with his usual flair for organisation that the most sensible idea would be for him to sit in the boudoir that opened out of Rania's bedroom.

She could then go in and show him each gown as soon as she had put it on.

Before he left the dining room he gave his precise instructions to his butler.

If anyone called to see him he was to say that he was not arriving in London until the evening.

He was sure that as soon as any of his relatives read the newspapers, they would come rushing round to find out what was going on and be extremely curious to see Rania.

He had not forgotten that he intended to find her a chaperone, someone of Social importance to be hostess at the luncheon and dinner parties he intended to give.

But again he did not want anyone to see Rania until he had dressed her.

The second shop arrived with as many attendants as the first and they were taken up to Rania's bedroom.

Charles climbed the stairs and entered the boudoir, a most attractive room with a comfortable sofa and several armchairs and a bookcase containing books that he knew would please Rania.

From their long discussions last night he was aware that her knowledge of history was almost as good as his.

He could not remember any of the women he had admired and made love to reading anything but the latest romantic novel and topical magazine or newspaper which mentioned themselves.

He seated himself comfortably in a leather armchair and as he did so the communicating door opened and Rania peeped inside.

"I wondered if you were in here," she called. "Are you ready for the parade?"

"I am waiting for it impatiently!"

She opened the door wide.

"Voila!" she cried, imitating one of

the *vendeuses* who was French.

She walked towards Charles wearing an extremely glamorous evening gown, thinking that it was much too spectacular to be worn except on the stage.

Rania had been quite right in thinking that fashion had altered. Gowns were considerably more elaborate than they had been during the war.

The cross-over bodice and the high waist, if there was one at all, were still in vogue, but now the fine muslin skirts, which for some years had been almost transparent, were embellished with flowers, lace or touches of velvet.

The neckline was still distinctly low.

This dress was a full kaleidoscope of colours and although Rania looked very attractive in it, Charles shook his head.

The Manageress was standing just inside the door.

"It is far too elaborate," Charles told her, "and the mass of colour just diminishes the purity of *mademoiselle's* skin and the colour of her hair."

The Manageress threw up her hands as if in despair.

Rania, walking back to the door, winked at Charles.

He recognised she was finding amusing the struggle between the two shops to sell their most expensive gowns.

There had been quite an argument in the bedroom as to which of the gowns should be presented first and the two Manageresses became quite heated.

Rania cleverly settled the question by making them throw some decorative dice she found on her mantelpiece.

They were larger than ordinary dice would be for a game of backgammon and were made of ebony and Rania had admired them last night when she was undressing.

She pressed them into the Manageresses' hands and they threw them onto the bed so as not to damage them.

The first Manageress threw numbers five and three and thought she would be the winner, but she was beaten by the other who threw six and four.

When Charles turned down the first gown, the other Manageress was delighted with the verdict and she helped Rania into what she now believed was the prettiest gown she had ever seen.

It was certainly unusual and was made of very soft material which Rania was sure came from Paris.

It was pure white but had something woven into it which gave the impression of moonlight when she moved.

The skirt was a little fuller than in the other gowns and it was decorated with tiny pale pink roses, all glittering with diamante-like dew-drops.

This decoration was almost entirely on the bottom of the skirt and only a few tiny roses were on the ribbons which crossed her in front and passed under Rania's small breasts.

The effect of the gown accentuated the perfection and slimness of her figure and was in every way different from the gown she had put on first.

As she walked into the boudoir she was not certain what Charles would say.

He took one look at her and knew at once that this was exactly what he wanted.

Although Rania was unaware of it, the gown made her look ethereal and spiritual and it was this that made her so different from the other women in London.

Charles did not say anything, but merely nodded to the Manageress, who was peeping around the doorway and clapped her hands in excitement.

Later he chose seven more evening gowns and then they started on gowns to be worn during the day.

Rania had learned the prices of some of the dresses he was buying and when she next came into the room in an attractive gown with a pretty little bonnet to match, she ran across the room.

She reached Charles before the Manageress came to the doorway.

"These lovely gowns are so terribly expensive," she whispered. "Please do not buy me any more. I am sure we can find a shop where they are cheaper."

Charles smiled.

"If you were riding Dragonfly in a race, would you put a cheap bridle on him and an uncomfortable saddle?"

"I know what you are saying," she laughed, "and at the same time I am trying to protect you from yourself."

Charles did not reply to her. He merely nodded to the Manageress and Rania walked back to change again.

Finally he said she had enough to be going on with and Rania sat down in a chair beside him.

"I feel even more exhausted than if I had galloped a hundred miles on Dragonfly," she sighed.

Charles put his hand up to his forehead.

"I had forgotten! You will need a riding habit."

"I am sure these women will have nothing like that in their shops," she murmured. "Or if they have, they will have little roses in silk around the collar and undoubtedly the riding boots will be made of velvet!"

Charles chuckled.

"It will not be as bad as that, but it has to be smart, otherwise Dragonfly might be ashamed of you!"

He walked into the next room to speak to the two Manageresses, who were now packing up the gowns he had refused to buy from them and the three of the gowns which needed small alterations.

As they told Charles, Rania was so slim that their model gowns had fitted as if they had been made for her.

He now ordered her two riding habits, one from each shop and both Manageresses were delighted. They left smiling at such a successful morning's business.

Charles went back to Rania who had put her feet up on another chair.

"I had never known that being fashionable could be so exhausting!" she exclaimed.

"You have only just started. Wait

until you have danced until three o'clock in the morning for at least seven days, and then, as I shall require of you, ride with me at seven o'clock in the morning in Rotten Row."

"I can see you were a real slave-driver in your last incarnation. And if I am a failure and you send me back to the country, I cannot think what you will do with all those glorious dresses."

She spoke without thinking and then she added,

"I expect you have a lovely lady friend who will be only too pleased to accept them."

She was speaking innocently.

Without having the slightest idea, he realised, what interpretation might be put on what she had said, he could, in fact, think of several 'lovely lady friends' who would be delighted to be given such beautiful gowns.

But it was one subject he would not be discussing with Rania.

It was time for luncheon and they went downstairs for another enjoyable meal.

They laughed and argued through every course.

A discussion was started by Rania, who wondered which century had produced the most beautiful clothes for women.

She was much in favour of mediaeval long sleeves and lofty headdresses, while Charles chose the Elizabethan age as being very feminine and attractive.

Then they talked of what the men wore with Rania expressing the view that the modern fashion was rather dull and Charles firmly insisting that men today had never been smarter or better looking.

"What I think now," he said, "is that men look like gentlemen and you must not forget that our host tonight is known as 'The First Gentleman of Europe'."

Rania stared at him.

"Who is — our host tonight?" she asked unsteadily.

"Oh, did I forget to tell you?" he replied, casually. "His Royal Highness the Prince Regent has invited us to dinner."

"I don't believe it! You are teasing

me!"

"No, it is the truth, Rania. He has always been very kind to me and when I told him that we were engaged to be married, he wished to be the first in London to meet you."

Rania sat staring at him wide-eyed.

"I brought in the morning newspapers which you will see are here beside me. Our engagement is announced in every one of them, including *The Gazette.*"

Rania gave a little cry.

"Why did — you not — tell me?"

"I am telling you now!"

She opened up the newspaper and found the Court column.

Charles watched her as she stood by the window with the sunshine glinting on her hair.

He hoped Silver was reading the same newspaper and she would feel, he was sure, as if she had received a slap in the face.

It would certainly be a shock for her and it would come as a great surprise for a number of other people.

'I have been very smart,' he said to himself. 'Silver will soon be licking her wounds.'

He had forbidden Rania to go outside the front door in case she was seen, so they walked into the garden at the back of the house after luncheon and sat under the trees.

There was a fountain with its exquisitely carved bowl throwing its water high up into the sky.

Wearing one of her new gowns Rania stood looking at the water, which turned into little rainbows as it fell.

'It is not only her beautiful face,' Charles thought. 'She has a grace in every movement she makes.'

She somehow reminded him of the statues of Greek Goddesses he had seen in Athens.

'She is, of course, exquisite,' he told himself. 'But her beauty grows on one just like a magic spell. I find her lovelier now than she seemed only a little while ago.'

They went back to the house for tea and the butler told Charles quite a number of people had called.

He had told them, as he had been ordered, that Mr. Lyndon was not arriving until the evening.

Listening, Rania realised that many of the callers had been Charles's relatives.

"I am certain that your aunts and cousins will all be most annoyed that they were not the first to meet me."

"Of course they will, but they know that we cannot refuse a Royal command!"

Rania put her head to one side.

"You have an answer for every-thing," she sighed. "However I have a suspicion that you have contrived this dinner party tonight in some clever way of you own."

"You are being far too perceptive,

Rania. I just like women to do exactly as I tell them and not to ask too many awkward questions."

"Nonsense!" she retorted. "You are too intelligent for that. You would surely be so bored stiff if everything went off exactly as you planned. If nothing else, this party tonight will be a surprise."

Charles realised she was even more perceptive than he had first thought.

"All right, Rania, you win. It is a surprise, not only for my family, but also for the young woman who did not think I was good enough for her."

Rania's eyes twinkled.

"So you *really* are punishing her. I am beginning to feel rather sorry for her already!"

"She will be a great deal sorrier for herself in a few days time."

Rania waited for his explanation and when he did not say anymore, she did not ask the obvious questions.

As Antonio was about to come to arrange her hair, she went up to her bedroom immediately they had finished tea.

The bath had been placed for her on the hearthrug and she thought how delightful it was to have two maids waiting on her.

The bath water was sprinkled with oil of lilies and the maids then dressed her except for the moonlight gown.

Antonio was announced.

He was a good-looking Italian now getting on in years. He had worked his way up to the top to become the most respected and the most expensive hairdresser in the whole of the *Beau Monde.*

He had been told by Major Monsell that he was wanted at Lyndon House to dress the hair of a young lady for whom His Royal Highness was giving a party.

He was filled with curiosity as he knew all about Charles Lyndon.

He had arranged the hair for many beautiful ladies who thought their hearts were broken because he had left them. He had expected, like everyone else in London, that the most dashing buck of St. James's Street was about to announce his engagement to the stunning Silver Bancroft.

When he had read in the morning newspapers that Charles Lyndon was to be married to someone different, he was astonished.

Every lady whose hair he had done today had been surprised and curious.

"Who can this young woman be, Antonio?" they all enquired. "No one I know has ever seen her. It seems amazing that someone as famous for his love affairs as Charlie to marry an unknown creature from the country."

There was a touch of spite in most of them.

Antonio guessed that Charles had either left them after a very short *affaire-de-coeur* or had paid no attention to them at all.

He was therefore bursting with curiosity when he arrived at Lyndon House.

He was escorted upstairs to Rania's bedroom.

When she rose to greet him from the stool in front of the dressing table, Antonio was astonished.

Knowing so much about Charles, he had been quite certain his future bride would be attractive.

The young lady holding out her hand to him had her strange fire-touched fair hair falling over her shoulders.

She was, Antonio knew at once, different from any lady acclaimed a current beauty in the *Beau Monde.*

"It is so kind of you to come to do my hair," Rania was saying in her soft voice. "My fiancé tells me that you are the very best hairdresser in the whole of London."

"I hope that is my reputation, *signorina*," Antonio replied. "But you shall tell me of your opinion of my work when I have arranged your hair."

Rania sat down just a little nervously in front of the mirror on the dressing table.

She was a little afraid that Antonio would make her look too different, but he was a real artist and he knew he had to accentuate something special in this lovely creature.

First he brushed her hair firmly until it shone and its strange Michelangelo lights glittered almost mystically.

Then he arranged it very carefully in what was the latest fashion and at the same time he made Rania's hair a halo for her heart-shaped face.

He had almost finished when there was a knock on the door and Charles came in.

"Good evening, Antonio," he began. "I have come to see what you have created. I never cease to be surprised at your skill with even a plain woman."

"Tonight, *signore,* you have presented me a beauty beyond all beauties and I have made her look as she looked when she was sitting on Mount Olympus."

Charles smiled.

It was just what he had thought himself.

Rania did have the look of a Greek Goddess and it pleased him that Antonio should have thought the same.

"Now I am feeling shy," said Rania. "But I hope, you are pleased, Charles."

She turned round and Charles knew that Antonio had used his brilliant talent in the way only he could use it.

Rania was looking exquisitely lovely and lovelier than she had looked even before. The elegance of her hair framed her face and made her beauty almost breathtaking.

"I told you Antonio was a genius and I have never seen you look more glorious."

Rania's eyes lit up.

"That is just what I wanted you to say."

"What I have brought you now," Charles continued, carrying a box in his hand, "is the jewellery you must wear, and I do not know if Antonio wants a piece for your hair?"

"Let me have a look at the gown Miss Temple will be wearing."

The maid who was standing by the door moved to the wardrobe and brought out the moonlight dress on its hanger and held it up for Antonio to see.

From the light of the candles,

which had now been lit because the sun was sinking, the dewdrops on the roses glittered like diamonds.

Antonio looked at the gown and then at the jewel-box which Charles held in his hands.

He had opened it and on the top velvet layer there were several brooches of diamonds.

Antonio picked up one of them and placed it on top of Rania's head where he had arranged a pile of curls.

"I like that effect," affirmed Charles.

"So do I, *signore*."

"What I have for your neck," suggested Charles, "is a small diamond necklace, because we are not yet married. But the diamonds are very special and will shine like your eyes and your gown."

He clasped a narrow necklace of diamonds around her neck. It was set at the front with a rose of the same stones from which fell a number of small diamond drops.

It was a pretty and unusual necklace with a similar bracelet and as Charles had known, it was exactly right for a young lady who was engaged to be married, but who was not yet wearing the wedding ring on her finger.

Charles next ushered Antonio into the boudoir and Rania dressed in the moonlight gown, which looked even more magical at night than it had in the morning.

The housekeeper had come in to

help and she was overwhelmed at how marvellous Rania looked.

"You'll be 'the belle of the ball', as they all says, miss," she told Rania. "And that's saying something when you're going to Carlton House."

"I am looking forward to seeing it and I hear it is very impressive."

"You're in for a real treat, that's what you are," the housekeeper said. "There's not any soul who's not come back from there and says they've never seen nothing like it in all their born days!"

"I am sure I will say the same."

She took one last look at herself in the mirror and carrying a chiffon handkerchief in her hand which matched her gown she walked into the boudoir.

The two men who had been talking turned round as she entered.

For a moment they were silent.

She walked towards them and Charles felt she had excelled in all he could have hoped for.

Antonio knew that the unique style in which he had dressed Rania's hair would be the talk of Mayfair.

Charles looked at the clock.

"Now we must go. Thank you very much, Antonio, and I hope, as I expect, we shall need you every day in the coming weeks, you will not refuse to arrange Rania's hair again. Otherwise she will just have to stay at home!"

"That would be a major catastrophe! Don't worry, *signore,* I will be here whenever you want me."

As Rania held out her hand, he kissed it.

Then he swaggered downstairs ahead of them well aware he had reached a new height of brilliance which he had not touched before.

Driving towards Carlton House, Charles remarked,

"I am wondering what His Royal Highness might have for us tonight. He thinks up all sorts of different ways of intriguing and fascinating his guests."

"I read that his party for the Duke of Wellington was wonderful."

"It certainly had everyone gasping. On the day of the fête, vast banks of artificial flowers were arranged on the floor in the shape of a temple."

"But why?" asked Rania.

"Behind a wall of petals and foliage were concealed two bands."

Rania laughed.

"That must have been quite a surprise."

"There was a large Corinthian temple in the garden, where the guests could admire a marble bust of the Duke."

"He must have been so pleased."

"He was so very delighted and the Prince Regent himself appeared in his Field Marshal's full dress uniform, wearing all his English, Russian, Prussian and Portuguese Orders!"

"I am sure he enjoyed every moment of it."

"So did the two thousand invited guests," continued Charles. "Even the Queen did not sit down to supper until two o'clock and stayed on until half-past four."

Rania gave a little cry.

"I hope we shall not be expected to do so tonight!"

"You never know what the Prince Regent will think of next, but I think actually as you are the star of the show and he only knew you were coming yesterday afternoon, we must not expect too much."

"I shall be quite content," sighed Rania, "to see the inside of Carlton House itself. I have read so much about it, but I have never thought I should actually be able to see it for myself."

"I shall be very interested to hear what you think not only of the house but of its owner."

When they arrived at Carlton House Charles sensed that Rania was feeling nervous.

When they walked slowly up the long staircase, he took her hand in his and found it trembling a little.

The Prince Regent was receiving his guests in the Chinese room. He had spent so much money and effort on it that he liked to use it for important occasions.

Despite the stoutness of his figure, he was looking exceedingly smart and the genial way he eagerly welcomed Charles was most endearing.

"I have been waiting for you, Charles," he called, "and you have my heartiest congratulations."

"I thank Your Royal Highness. May I present my fiancée, Miss Rania Temple."

Rania sank down to the ground in a deep curtsy.

The Prince Regent looked at her and exclaimed,

"Lovely! Exquisite! You are so right, Charles, she will wipe the eye of every beauty strutting about in London like an important peahen!"

"I was hoping that was what you would say, Sire."

The Prince Regent had taken Rania's hand in his.

"How could Charles have found

anyone so glorious and so unusual," he asked, "in what I hear is
the depths of the country?"

"He just appeared completely
unexpectedly, Your Royal Highness," replied Rania. "But I think it
must have been genuine fate that
directed him to our door because
his horse had cast a shoe."

The Prince Regent laughed.

"So that was how you met."

"Actually if you would like the
whole story," came in Charles, "I
first met Rania when she was only
eight and have been in love with
her ever since!"

The Prince Regent thought this
was amusing and he clapped
Charles on the shoulder.

Then as there was a queue of

guests behind them, who had just arrived, they moved away.

"Don't take your beauty too far, Charles," said the Prince Regent. "She is sitting next to me at dinner and I shall have a great deal to say to her."

Charles recognised that no one could ever achieve a better entrance into the Social world.

When they moved into the drawing room everyone rushed towards him and Rania as they wished to make the acquaintance of the new beauty of the *Beau Monde.*

Rania, Charles found, having been put at her ease by the Prince Regent was no longer nervous.

She accepted the compliments the gentlemen paid to her and she managed to evade the questions asked by the curious ladies.

There had been only a short time for the Prince to organise his party, so tonight there would be no fireworks, but Japanese lanterns hung from every tree in the garden.

In the dining room there was one large round table and several smaller ones to accommodate the sixty guests who had been invited for this special occasion.

The Prince Regent as usual had come up a new idea.

The whole room was decorated with white flowers and most of them had been sprinkled with diamante.

Especially those on the polished table, which was an innovation introduced by His Royal Highness himself.

It was almost, Charles thought, as if he had known clairvoyantly what Rania would be wearing.

She sparkled with the diamonds round her neck and the diamante on her moonlight gown.

And so did the white flowers glitter and small lights were hidden amongst flowers arranged in the room to give an impression of a white fairyland.

No one had ever seen such scenic effects anywhere.

"It is all so lovely, Your Royal Highness," enthused Rania excitedly, as she sat down beside him. "How could you think of anything so original?"

"I try always to think of new ideas, my dear. As you are so new to the London scene it is only right that you should be given a display that as far as I know no beautiful woman has ever been treated to before."

"It is something I shall always remember and from what I have already seen of your marvellous house, it is even more exciting than I thought it would be."

"I shall take you round myself," he suggested. "And you must tell me what you think about all my latest purchases which I have not yet even shown to Charles."

"I should love to, Your Royal Highness. Please do not forget that is what you have promised me."

"How could I ever forget anything I have promised you?" asked the Prince Regent. "It is not often I entertain a Goddess from Olympus!"

Rania thought it was very probably something he might have said before, but she was so delighted to be paid such a handsome compliment.

'When I tell Harry what he has just said to me,' she thought, 'he will *never* believe me.'

She felt sad that her brother was not here after all they had been through, but she was certain he was enjoying every moment at Lyndon Hall designing the Racecourse for Charles.

It was what he had always wanted

himself and yet he believed it was one of those impossible dreams which could never come true.

'This too is a dream,' Rania mused, looking around the room.

It was all thanks to Charles.

As she saw him laughing and talking halfway down the table, she sensed he was enveloped by a bright light.

The light of the Gods which the Prince Regent had tried to conjure up with his roses.

'He is so wonderful,' she said to herself. 'I am just frightened he may disappear and I will wake up and find that this is all an unbelievable dream.'

CHAPTER FIVE

As they drove back home in the early hours of the morning Rania talked excitedly about the evening.

It was not surprising.

First they had enjoyed a dinner of many courses, all delectable.

Then they had gone into the garden and there they had watched many graceful and agile dancers, all dressed in white, springing over the lawn and the flower beds.

Some were lithe gymnastic dancers who were lifted up into the air and they seemed almost to touch the stars.

The music was extremely beautiful and when they had finished to rapturous applause, the orchestra continued by playing romantic tunes accompanied by singers hidden behind great banks of flowers.

Everything was pure white and everything seemed to shimmer in the light of the moon rising up in the sky.

"It was certainly something entirely new," Charles commented as they drove back to Berkeley Square. "And all London will be talking about the party tomorrow."

He paused and then added,

"And specially about *you* —"

"I did nothing spectacular,"

sighed Rania.

"But the party was all for you and everyone thought you were as beautiful as the white roses. In the garden you seemed to become part of the moonlight."

"That is a most romantic thing to say. I only hope I can live up to it."

"Wait and see —" murmured Charles.

And as they reached Berkeley Square, he said,

"I know you want to ride with me in Rotten Row, but tomorrow morning as soon as we have eaten breakfast we must start our round of visits to my relatives, otherwise they will be very annoyed with me for neglecting them."

"Then of course we must go to

them first."

She started up the stairs and then as Charles did not follow her, she stopped to lean over the banisters, calling,

"Thank you! Thank you so much again, Charles. This evening is something I shall always remember."

He smiled at her and she waved as she ran further up the stairs.

He thought as he went to his study that the evening had been an even bigger success than he could have hoped.

There was a long list on his writing table that Major Monsell had prepared for him. It was of all his relatives who lived in London and their addresses.

Charles thought with a groan it was going to take a long time to see them all, but he knew it had to be done.

Rania was finding it difficult to sleep because she was still so excited.

She was thinking that the Prince Regent was one of the most charming men she had ever met.

He had paid her a number of effusive compliments when she had said goodbye, but she did not entirely believe them.

She considered it was wonderful of him to take so much trouble over her, but no one could be any kinder or so marvellous as Charles.

She thanked God for him again in her prayers and also included the

Prince Regent.

Then she lay wide awake for ages seeing all the dancers, the lanterns and the decorations in the ballroom and again Charles.

She had paid very little attention to the other guests as she was frightened that if she talked to anyone for long they would ask her awkward questions.

There had been several young gentlemen who had said how delighted they were to meet her and looking back she could not remember their faces or their names.

Finally when at last she fell into a deep sleep it was to dream she was dancing in the garden with the dancers.

■ ■ ■ ■

The next morning after a maid had helped Rania to dress, she hurried downstairs for breakfast, feeling a little afraid that Charles might be angry if she was late.

She had dressed in what she decided was one of the prettiest of the day gowns he had bought for her and she carried the matching bonnet.

When she walked into the dining room Charles was already eating breakfast and reading a newspaper propped up on a silver stand.

"Good morning to you, Rania. You are late! I have a feeling that if Dragonfly was expecting you, you would not have kept him waiting!"

"I am sorry, but I took longer than usual in dressing because I knew I had to look my best for your relatives."

"What you ought to worry about is the number of questions they are going to ask you. Just stick to the story of how we met when you were eight and let them think we have been in communication with each other ever since."

"I am not good at telling lies, Charles."

She was helping herself to bacon and eggs from one of the silver dishes on the sideboard.

"Then don't think of it as a lie," he replied sharply. "This is just a game anyone might play and I keep thinking of how much Harry is enjoying himself."

Rania realised he thought that she was complaining.

Carrying her plate, she sat down beside him.

"Please," she began, "try to remember I am just a stupid little maid who has lived amongst the cabbages and weeds for the last five years. I know nothing of the smart world you have brought me into."

She made her pleading sound pathetic and Charles instinctively relaxed.

"If I seem unkind, Rania, you must forgive me. It is just that so much depends on the act we are playing that even I am feeling a little apprehensive!"

"You said yourself it is just a game

in which we are trying to help others as well as ourselves, so only think of that."

"You are very sensible, Rania. Now, if you have had enough to eat, let us start our task of bringing sunshine and happiness to my relations, who are thinking they have been ignored."

Rania drank her coffee and rose from the table.

She picked up her bonnet and put it on in front of a gold mirror.

It was certainly most becoming and because it was in the same pale blue colour of her eyes, it made her skin seem almost dazzlingly white.

Then Charles opened the door and they walked into the hall to find a phaeton waiting outside for them drawn by two perfectly matched horses.

It was a comfortable size and not too high, but even so, Rania had to climb into it carefully in case she dirtied her new gown against the wheel.

The groom next jumped in and they drove off.

Rania stole a sideways glance at Charles to see if he was still in a difficult mood.

She thought, with his tall hat a little on one side of his head, he looked very dashing.

She was certain that the women they passed as they drove down Piccadilly would be envious of her.

The first relation they called on was Charles's aunt, his mother's sister, and she was the one he wanted to come to Lyndon House to chaperone Rania.

Lady Salford was getting on for sixty, but was still good-looking. She had been a widow for some years and now she spent a great deal of time working for charities, especially those that raised money for poor children.

She was a very gentle lady with a charm that made her popular with every generation.

Charles had considered that there was no one more suitable to chaperone Rania and was only afraid his Aunt Margaret would refuse.

They arrived at her house in Belgrave Square and when they were shown into the drawing room Lady

Salford was sitting at her writing table.

She rose with a cry of delight.

"Charles! My dear boy, I was just writing a letter to you. I only managed to see the announcement of your engagement in the newspaper yesterday evening."

"I am sorry I could not let you know before, Aunt Margaret, but I was in the country persuading Rania to come to London and there was really no way of getting in touch with you."

He kissed his aunt as he spoke and then he said,

"This is Rania and she is the sister of Harry Temple who you may remember has been my friend since we were at Eton together."

"Yes, of course I remember, dear boy."

She took Rania's hands in both of hers.

"You are very like your mother, who was one of the sweetest people I ever knew."

Rania gave a little cry.

"You knew Mama? Oh, how wonderful!"

"I knew you mother even before she married your father," explained Lady Salford. "And if you are as sweet as she was, then Charles is indeed a very lucky man."

"I would love to talk to you about Mama. I miss her so much and because I have been living in the depths of the country, there was no one I could talk to about her."

"That is exactly what I would like to do, Rania."

Charles knew that this was his opportunity.

"I have not only brought Rania to meet you, Aunt Margaret, but I am on my knees begging for your help."

"My help! What has gone wrong?"

"Nothing is at all wrong, but we have just arrived in London and Rania has no chaperone. Mrs. Monsell, my secretary's wife, looked after her last night, but I must have one of the family for the job to be done properly."

"And you want me?"

"Of course I want you, Aunt Margaret. You have always been my most favourite relative, although you must not tell the others. And as you knew Rania's mother that makes everything perfect."

"Then of course I will chaperone her. Do you want her to come here to me or shall I come to you?"

"As I intend to give some large parties, perhaps a ball, I think it would be much easier if you came to Lyndon House."

"Then it is just what I will do, dear boy, but I shall have to bring my secretary as well as my lady's maid with me. I have so many plans for one of my charities, which I cannot set on one side."

"No problem, Aunt Margaret. It will be wonderful to have you to stay with me and thank you so much for being so understanding."

He kissed his aunt's cheek.

She promised to move to Lyndon House as soon as she could organise her packing.

They left Lady Salford and she assured Rania that they would have a great many things to talk about.

As they drove off Rania remarked,

"By the expression in your voice I could tell how pleased you were. I think your aunt is most charming and I shall be very happy talking to her about my Mama."

"I only hope you have time. We have a great deal to do."

"Why so much hurry?"

"I have found that things done briskly and quickly are always more satisfactory than if people drag their feet and get bored with the whole project."

The way he spoke to her gave Rania a sharp feeling as though someone had given her a stab in the heart.

Was it that he was already bored with the idea of presenting her to the *Beau Monde*?

Was there someone else he would rather be with?

She longed to ask him so many questions, but was afraid of the answers.

Next they called on a close cousin who considered herself very important and she was extremely annoyed that Charles had not informed her of his engagement before it appeared in the newspapers.

"Surely Charles," she began to

scold him harshly, "you must know better than to spring surprises on me in such an extraordinary manner. I hear as well that you took your fiancée to Carlton House last night."

"His Royal Highness was kind enough to give a party especially for Rania."

"It is most incorrect," his cousin retorted, "for her to appear anywhere in pubic until she had been introduced to the family."

"I know that, but I had to see His Royal Highness on business and when I told him I was engaged, he insisted on giving a dinner party for her the next evening. I could hardly refuse."

His cousin realised this was true

and relaxed a little.

At the same time she was not at all welcoming and as they drove away, Rania commented,

"I am afraid you upset her."

"Anything can. She is a tiresome woman and both my parents always avoided her if they could. However she could make mischief and I reckoned, although she would hate to admit it, that she was very impressed with you."

"Do you really think so? I was so scared of saying the wrong thing that I said very little."

"That is just what she liked as she always wishes to do all the talking and I never go near her if I can help it."

Rania laughed at this and then

they travelled on to the next names on the list.

They were mostly cousins, some because they were related to Charles's mother, the others to his father and they were all most curious, but very delighted that Charles had decided to settle down.

"We have been so very anxious for him to marry," one of them said to Rania. "But he is such a success with the ladies that he gives them up almost before we realise he was interested in them!"

Rania smiled.

"That must have made things rather difficult."

"It did indeed," agreed the relative.

Charles was on the other side of

the room talking to another member of the family, so the relative lowered her voice to say,

"We want him to settle down and have a family and of course he could be happy under those circumstances at Lyndon Hall. It is too big for a bachelor alone, but I feel sure he will be content there once he has a wife."

She waited for Rania to answer and she could only murmur,

"I hope I will make him — a good one."

They visited six more relatives and took luncheon with the last one.

When they left Charles said they had done enough.

"If you are not worn out," he said.

"I am! I am sick of saying the same words over and over again. But you have been marvellous and it pleased me greatly to see the admiration in their eyes when they first saw you."

"I thought they were just being critical."

"Not a bit of it, Rania, you are exactly what they want for me. As I expect you noticed, they all asked when the wedding is to take place as they are afraid that I shall run out on you at the last moment!"

Rania drew in her breath.

"And that is exactly what — you are going to do," she said in a small voice.

"Yes, of course," agreed Charles. "Then they will just have to start worrying about me all over again."

'It doesn't seem to worry him all that much,' Rania thought to herself.

She felt that his relatives loved him and were very proud of his bravery in the war and when they learned that he was not going to be married after all they would be most upset.

It was going to be very difficult for him to explain why he no longer wished to be married.

Because he guessed what she was thinking, Charles said sharply,

"Stop worrying! Something will turn up at the last moment which will make it easier than you think it will be. I am always lucky."

"I am keeping my fingers crossed —"

They were driving up Piccadilly.

At that moment in front of them a woman pushing a small boy in a handcart stepped off the pavement in order to cross the road.

She was also carrying a baby under one arm.

She had just reached the middle of the road when a phaeton drawn by three horses came tearing down the road.

It was being driven much too fast by a young buck who should have known better.

The woman, seeing its approach, tried to hurry out of the way, but one of the wheels of her handcart caught on a loose stone.

It tipped sideways and the little boy fell out.

It was only by an unexpected piece of good driving that the wheels of the buck's phaeton did not go over him.

The woman nearly fell as it passed her with only an inch or two to spare.

Charles pulled his horses to a standstill and before he could say a word Rania had leapt from the phaeton and was running towards the little boy.

He was crying tempestuously as she picked him up and said tenderly,

"It is all right, you are quite safe, no one has hurt you."

His mother was still holding the baby in her arms, but he must have been squeezed as she almost fell, so he too was crying.

Charles told his groom to pull the handcart onto the pavement as another vehicle might come hurtling down the road at any moment.

The small boy was still crying and Rania looked up at his mother.

"Shall I hold the baby so you can comfort the boy?"

The woman seemed incapable of saying anything so she handed Rania the baby who had now ceased crying.

"Let us move onto the pavement," suggested Rania. "We will be safer there."

The groom was already taking away the hand cart.

As the mother picked up her son

and followed him, Rania did the same.

She was looking down at the baby in her arms.

Watching her, Charles felt that she was a symbolic figure.

He was sure, although he could not see it, that there was a softness in her eyes and a faint smile on her lips as she looked at the child in her arms.

It occurred to him that it was what he would ask of any wife in the future who would bear his children — that she should love them protectively and adoringly because they were his and hers.

Now the mother had carried the little boy onto the pavement and he stopped crying and there were just some bruises on his knees.

As Rania passed the phaeton to reach the pavement, Charles called out,

"Ask that woman where she is going."

Rania asked the mother the question.

"Us be going to the 'ospital," she replied. "Baby's got trouble with his eye and there be a doctor a-waitin' to see us."

"Is that why you were in so much of a hurry?"

The woman nodded.

"If us be late for 'im, he takes 'is patients as they come and us might be there a long time."

She repeated to Charles what the woman had said.

He smiled at her.

"Then we must take them to the hospital. It will be a bit of a squeeze, but I am sure we can manage it."

Rania then helped the woman with the baby in her arms into the phaeton and sat her next to Charles.

Rania sat opposite with the little boy on her lap. He had stopped whimpering about his knees now that he was inside the phaeton.

As Charles drove off he blurted out,

"Big 'orses, Jimmy love big 'orses!"

"That be so true," said his mother. "He's been mad about 'orses ever since he could toddle."

"When you are bigger you will be able to ride a big stallion," Rania told the boy. "But before you do so, you must learn to talk to him."

"Talk to 'im? But will 'e be able to talk to me?" asked Jimmy looking puzzled.

"He will nuzzle up against you, which will show he understands. If you talk to him and pat him before you ride him, he will learn to do exactly what you want and he will love you as you love him."

Jimmy thought it over.

"I'll do that, miss," he stammered after a while.

"Do not forget what I have told you, because it is very important. When I talk to my horse, called Dragonfly, he understands everything I say to him."

"I'll talk to my 'orse, and I'll call him Jimmy after me."

"That is a very good idea."

Listening to her Charles thought she was behaving in a different way from any woman he had known and he had taken a great number of them driving with him.

He was more than certain that if there had been an accident, they would have been the first to avert their eyes and then they would have implored him to drive away as quickly as possible.

It was so like Rania to have him embroiled with a woman and two children he had never seen before and was unlikely to see again.

Yet when he thought about it, it

was exactly how his mother had always behaved and because she could not bear to see anyone suffering, she felt she had to help them however difficult it might be.

It did not take them long to reach the local hospital, which was off Oxford Street.

"Where do you live?" Charles asked the woman.

"Not far from the river, sir."

"It is a long way for you to have to walk with these children."

"Us'll manage it some'ow, sir."

"As Jimmy has hurt his knees, I think you should call a Hackney carriage to take you back home."

The woman did not answer and he realised she was thinking it was something they could not afford.

Charles now drew his horses to a standstill outside the hospital and before she could make a move, he placed three guineas into her hand.

As she stared at him in astonishment, he said,

"Take a Hackney carriage home and spend the rest on good food for your husband and the children."

"Thank you, sir, thank you!" she cried. "It's really kind of you."

Charles bent over her and put a half-sovereign into Rania's hand.

"Give it to Jimmy and tell him to spend it on some sweets for himself and a present for his mother."

When the groom lifted Jimmy down, Rania pressed the half-sovereign into his hand and told him what Charles had said.

"Sweeties!" exclaimed Jimmy. "I likes sweets."

"And a present for your Mama," insisted Rania.

"I'll do that."

"Say 'thank you' to the lady," called his mother.

Jimmy lifted up his arm and as Rania bent towards him, he put it round her neck and kissed her.

"Thank you, miss. I loves you very much."

"And I love you, Jimmy, I hope one day I will see you again."

"You've been ever so kind, miss," Jimmy's mother said to Rania.

"You have two lovely children and that is just what I hope I will have one day."

"I'm sure God'll bless you, miss."

Jimmy was clutching his half-sovereign very tightly in his hand and as they walked towards the hospital, Rania climbed back on to the phaeton.

"They are such sweet children," she sighed.

"And you were very sweet with them, Rania."

"So were you, Charles."

"I hoped you would approve," he smiled, "and if I go on like this, I shall take up good works and find myself eventually becoming a monk!"

Rania laughed.

"I am quite certain there would be a million women to save you from such a calling!"

Charles turned the horses towards

Berkeley Square and muttered to Rania,

"I consider we have done enough good deeds today to ensure us of a front seat in Heaven when we get there!"

"I doubt it is as easy as that. You know as well as I do there are still a great number of relatives on your list."

"We will do them tomorrow and after we have had tea, I am going to lie on the sofa with my feet up and read the newspapers."

Rania smiled, but she agreed with Charles that they had really done enough for one day.

"What is happening tonight?" she now asked.

"I thought that would occur to

you sooner or later. We are dining with a Duchess and going on to a ball given by a foreign Prince. And let me say you will have to be the most beautiful lady present at both these engagements."

"I think you are asking too much of me and if I am a disappointment, what will you do then?"

Charles did not reply.

"I know the answer already. I shall be sent back to the country in disgrace and you will tell your family I am dead!"

"You are talking a great deal of nonsense!" Charles protested. "It is a great mistake to put such ideas into my mind!"

"I am not at all sure that I am reading your thoughts correctly," she retorted. "I have had some most strange ones lately."

"Most women tell me that they dream about me."

"That is a great mistake. It makes you conceited. So I shall tell you tomorrow that I have dreamt of Apollo and he is very, very handsome!"

"It is strange you should say that — so many people have told me that I remind them of Apollo!"

"You are most incorrigible. Actually I am a little shocked at your being pleased with yourself. I am sure that one day, like Jimmy, you will have a nasty fall."

"I only hope that there is a beautiful angel looking exactly like you to pick me up!"

Rania made a gesture with her hands.

"It's no use, you always have the last word. So I just have to admit that you are the winner and I will do exactly what you want."

Charles chuckled to himself, thinking that only with Rania could he indulge in this type of conversation.

They enjoyed a really delicious tea of muffins and iced cakes and later walked into the study where Charles picked up the newspapers.

"Are you going to read here with me?" he asked, "or lie down upstairs?"

"I am far too young to lie down in the afternoon as old gentlemen like you do. I am going to the library to find some even more exciting books than I have already."

She left the study and Charles lay down on the sofa and opened *The Morning Post.*

As he did so a name caught his eye and he read on,

"Good news of the Duke of Oakenshaw.

It is with much pleasure that we can announce that His Grace the Duke of Oakenshaw, who has recently been so ill that his relatives had feared for his life, has made a miraculous recovery.

Following the suggestion of one of his sisters, the doctors have used herbs instead of their usual medicines.

In addition they prescribed iron of

which his body was seriously defi-
cient. His Grace has now recovered
his strength and is out of danger.

There is great rejoicing at Oaken-
shaw Castle and the Duke himself
has declared it is a miracle for which
he is exceedingly grateful."

Charles read it twice to make quite sure he was not mistaken and said to himself that fate had clearly punished Silver even more effectively than he was able to do.

He could just about guess at the disappointment of Wilfred Shaw, who was so obviously waiting to step into the title and the delight of the Duke's other relatives.

The Duke was, in fact, a comparatively young man, being just on fifty.

Charles was extremely interested in his being cured by herbal medicine as his mother had always been a great believer in iron.

He remembered when in France he had learned that if a man was almost dying, iron would often revive him.

The French nurses would often put a rusty nail into a glass of water and then later they made the patient drink the water.

It seemed so extraordinary, but he had been told by several soldiers the difference it had made to them and he expected something like that had happened to the Duke.

What he had read made him decide to see to it that the herb garden, which had been his mother's great delight at Lyndon Hall, was kept in good order.

Country folk passionately believed in the efficacy of herbal medicine and when he told Rania the story about the Duke's speedy recovery as they were driving towards their dinner-party, Rania said exactly the same.

"I call it very interesting. We have a herb garden at home, but I have spent little time in it. As you will know, Charles, we had to give up our gardeners."

"You must tell Harry to put it in order as soon as he has finished working for me at the Hall," insisted Charles.

"I am sure Harry will want to, but it will be a long time off. If he has to build your Racecourse and also see to anything you want done in the house, I think the Temple's home will remain neglected."

"You will have to talk to your brother about it, but I do agree that even he cannot do two jobs at the same time."

"I am not worrying. As soon as I return home I will see to it."

Charles glanced at her.

"Do you want to go so quickly?"

"No, of course not. But this exciting drama cannot go on for ever. I am being sensible enough to enjoy every minute of it and I will not whine when it all ends."

"If I have my way, Rania, it will not end for you. I told you I am going to find you a rich husband

and we will look round tonight to see if there is anyone you fancy."

Rania did not answer and after a moment he asked,

"Why are you so very quiet, Rania, why don't you say something?"

"I was just thinking," she replied. "Love does not happen like that."

"Like what?"

"If love is coming to you, it comes without seeking or hunting for it. That would belittle the importance of it, and to me love is very, very wonderful."

"But you have never been in love, Rania, so how do you know?"

"Papa and Mama loved each other in a way which was so very special and moving. It made everything they said and did seem to be part of the sunshine."

There was silence for a moment.

"It is very strange you should say that, because my father and mother too loved each other so very much and I was brought up in a house filled with love. I thought then, as I think now, it is what I really need in my own house."

He paused before he added,

"But I was so foolish and simple to be deceived by a woman I thought would bring that special love to me."

The bitterness in his voice was so unmistakable that instinctively Rania put out her hand to touch his.

"You are not to think of love like

that. It is so easy for a man to make a mistake, but you have been fortunate enough not to be trapped completely and to escape being married to someone who was not good enough for you."

Her fingers tightened for a moment on Charles's.

"I pray you will be happy and I do feel that one day you will find a woman who really loves you and who is the other half of yourself."

Charles realised that she was thinking of the ancient Greek belief that man when first created by God was one single person and because he was so lonely, God had cut him in half and called the other half 'woman'.

She was the soft, sweet, gentle

and spiritual side of their love.

This is what every man and woman who followed them were seeking and when they found the other half of themselves they were one person and happy for all eternity.

Charles could remember his mother telling him the story when he was small and he thought it very touching that Rania should refer to it.

"You are so right, Rania, that is the perfection we all hope for and try to find. Perhaps one day both you and I will be lucky."

"I am sure we shall be," she replied taking away her hand. "And the people who disappoint and fail us are not worth thinking about."

Charles gave a little chuckle.

"I do get the message. Tonight we will be enjoying ourselves and perhaps the two partners we are seeking will drop down the chimney or fall from the ceiling!"

"In which case we will not be able to recognise them as they will be covered with soot and plaster!"

They were laughing together as they arrived at the house where they were to dine.

CHAPTER SIX

Rania and Charles were riding back from Rotten Row, leaving behind a crowd of young men who waited every morning to ride beside Rania and to be able to boast that they had done so.

As they turned into Berkeley Square, Rania said,

"Dragonfly would love to race against you and your best stallion in the country."

Charles looked at her.

"Are you bored already with being the beauty of all the beauties?"

Rania laughed.

"It is not that. It is just that we have so much to do that I no longer have those exciting conversations with you when we duelled with each other in words."

Charles smiled.

"Shall I tell you what you are doing today?"

"Yes, tell me."

"We are having luncheon, as you know, with the Duchess and I think you should look quite seriously at the Duke's eldest son."

Rania did not reply as he continued,

"This evening we will be dining at the House of Lords as the guests of the Earl and Countess of Staghurst. I expect we shall be on the terrace, so although you must wear one of your best evening gowns, it should not be too *décolleté.*"

"It sounds very interesting," she murmured, without much enthusiasm in her voice.

"If you are an extra good girl I have a surprise for you tomorrow which I think you will enjoy."

"What is it?" she enquired now sounding interested.

"I have a yacht called the *Mermaid.*"

"A yacht! That is very smart! But I thought only Americans owned yachts."

"That is true. They have had them since 1717 and when I heard about some of the biggest and fastest yachts we were already at war. I was, however, determined when peace came to buy one for myself."

"It sounds most exciting," sighed Rania. "I would love to see it."

"I thought we should take the day off and we will leave early tomorrow morning. We can sail down as far as the sea before we have to come back and inevitably go to another ball."

"It is the most thrilling idea. I have never seen the sea and I have never been in a ship."

"Then it will be a new experience for you. I assure you the *Mermaid* is very beautiful. At least I think so!"

"Oh, I do wish it was tomorrow already," enthused Rania. "I would

273

much rather be on your yacht than going to the House of Lords."

"You will find it a most fascinating place. If you marry a Lord, you will undoubtedly have to spend a great deal of time in the rather gloomy chamber and in the even drearier dining room!"

Rania giggled.

"You are obviously trying to depress me, Charles, but so far, let me point out, no Lord has proposed to me."

"I thought that young man last night was being very ardent."

"He was, but he is not a Lord and I think there are two of three brothers between him and his father's title."

"Then of course he must come

off the list," Charles added somewhat sarcastically.

"I have told you over and over
again that I have no wish to marry
anyone for their title or their
money."

"We will wait and see," said
Charles enigmatically.

They had arrived back in Berkeley
Square and two grooms were waiting to take the horses.

Rania now had to hurry to change
for the luncheon party.

She smiled at Charles and as she
did so he thought how attractive
she looked.

He was not surprised that she had
so many admirers in Rotton Row.

In fact he had ordered two more
riding habits for her as it was im-

possible, now that she was acclaimed as a beauty, for her to appear in the same clothes day after day.

The habit she was wearing he had admired as soon as she came down to breakfast.

It was leaf-green with white braiding on the jacket and her little tricorne hat was also green and very attractive.

'There is no doubt,' he thought, as he walked to his study, 'that it has paid to dress her'.

As usual there was a good number of letters waiting for him on his writing desk as Major Monsell was most intuitive in recognising those he should open himself and those which were private.

Now that he was supposedly engaged to be married, the private pile was growing smaller, but in the last several days since the announcement that the Duke of Oakenshaw had recovered, he had received three letters in writing he recognised.

He knew only too well that as Silver's engagement to the Marquis had not yet been proclaimed, she would try to get hold of him again.

He had looked at the letters when they arrived and then without opening them he put them in an envelope and returned them to Silver.

He had thought it was typical of her conceit.

She really believed after the appalling way she had behaved that he would take her back into his life.

The luncheon with the Duchess was very much like the other luncheons they had attended lately. There were the same *beaux* and bucks who rushed straight for Rania the moment they arrived.

She soon realised they were paying her the same compliments she had received from them at every other meeting.

The women as usual were inclined to be wary of her and those Charles had favoured in the past fawned on him or else they turned away from him when he entered the room and deliberately avoided him all through the party.

As the luncheon dragged on

Charles found himself thinking that Rania had been right.

She had said the conversation was boring as it did not have the sparkle and originality of the discussions they enjoyed when they were alone.

When he made yet another witty remark he found himself wishing that Rania could answer it, rather than the woman he was talking to.

As they returned to his home in the phaeton, Rania commented,

"I thought that was an extremely dull party. I kept thinking how exciting it will be tomorrow."

"As you are now the beauty of the Season, you are supposed to enjoy the luncheons and dinners given in your honour, even though the host-ess pretends she would have given it anyway."

"Now you are really flattering me!"

"It is, as it happens, the truth, Rania. They know if they invite you all of the most fastidious young aristocrats will accept their invitations so that they can flirt with you."

"If you ask me, the whole thing is ridiculous. It is just because you have dressed me up like a fairy Princess and Antonio has made the way he arranges my hair the new fashion."

She smiled at him before she went on,

"It is, of course, most flattering, but you know as well as I do that without Lyndon Hall, no one would have given me a second glance."

Charles knew she was right and he thought it was so like Rania to be modest enough to say so.

"I like you," he said, "as you are and whatever you are wearing. I am sure that is what Dragonfly thinks too!"

"Of course he does as so would any sensible human being!"

She gave a little sigh.

"I think it is rather sad that clothes matter so much to these people. That is, if you can afford them!"

"I am not stopping you from putting on all your old rags and tatters, but just think how disappointed all those elegant young men would be."

"Half the time," she laughed, "they are just thinking about their own appearance rather than mine. But I am not ungrateful for what you have done — you do know that."

She was thinking of the most enthusiastic letter she had just received from Harry, who had told her that he had found the ideal place for the new Racecourse and he would send Charles suggested plans for it in a few days.

'We have been so very, very lucky,' Rania thought when she read his letter. 'What more could I want?'

Then as the answer to her question came flooding into her head she quickly tried to brush it away.

She forced herself to think of something else.

They had been invited to be at the House of Lords by seven o'clock.

"Surely that is very early?" remarked Rania.

"It is usual when you are asked to dine at the Houses of Parliament in the summer for the guests to go onto the terrace to admire the Thames and have a drink before they go into the dining room."

"I shall love that, as I have always heard the view from the terrace is most attractive."

"It is indeed and tomorrow when we sail past it you will have a different view of Parliament from the Thames."

"You are making it sound quite an adventure!"

As Charles had suggested, she put on one of her very prettiest dresses, but it was, however, not so *décolleté* as her other evening gowns.

It was ornamented with tiny rows of lace round the bottom of the skirt with similar rows on the sleeves.

It made her, Charles thought when he saw her, look very young as well as enchanting and ethereal.

Antonio had prepared her hair in a softer fashion than usual.

Rania thought it would be too ostentatious to wear diamonds for such an occasion, so she therefore merely put a simple pearl necklace round her neck and wore no other jewellery except her engagement ring.

"Do I look all right?" she asked Charles when she went downstairs.

It was a question she had asked him every night just in case she might be wearing something he did not approve of or which did not, in his words, 'come up to scratch'.

"You look lovely and very feminine," he said. "All the elderly Lords, and some of them are very decrepit, will be pursuing you!"

Rania laughed and held up her hands.

"I do hope not!"

When they arrived at the House of Lords, they were escorted by a red-coated servant to the terrace, where the Countess, who was almost sixty, was receiving the guests with her husband, who was at least fifteen years older.

Charles knew her well and after she had greeted him and he had introduced Rania, she said,

"General Wallis is longing to talk to you, so be a good boy and spend a little time with him. He is sitting at the far end of the terrace because he is suffering badly with his gout and cannot move about easily."

"I will go to talk to him," Charles promised.

He had served under General Wallis in the Army and had great respect for him and he was well aware that the General was very fond of him.

They had arrived punctually at

the House of Lords and yet the terrace seemed already to be full with elegant ladies and somewhat aged gentlemen.

The servants were carrying around trays of drinks.

Charles took a glass of champagne but Rania shook her head.

She did not really like alcohol and she thought also that with so much to remember, it would be a mistake for her to drink anything that might affect her brain.

As soon as they moved away from the Countess, Charles was hailed by a number of his friends most of them older than himself and they all wanted to meet Rania.

Remembering what the Countess had asked him to do, Charles

gradually edged Rania towards the end of the terrace, where he found the old General seated on a low chair with one gouty leg stuck out in front of him.

"How are you, sir?"

"I have been waiting to see you, Charles. Introduce me to the young lady you are going to marry. I suppose she knows you will be a handful for her to look after!"

"I have told her how brave she is to take me on!"

"Well, I can really only admire your taste," said the General, as he shook hands with Rania. "You are a very lucky man."

"I do know, sir," agreed Charles.

"And I am lucky too," Rania piped up. "I am very proud of the medals Charles won during the war."

"He would have been awarded more than two if I had anything to do with it," said the General. "He is brave, and he has common sense, which is more than most of the young jackanapes have today!"

Rania smiled and sat down beside him.

There was only one chair and Charles began to look around for another.

As he did so, he saw someone edging through the crowd towards them.

It was Silver.

He had forgotten, rather stupidly, that the Countess of Staghurst was a relative of Silver's mother.

If he had been sensible, he would have refused this invitation.

He felt sure that if Silver was introduced to Rania, she would be rude, which would be uncomfortable, or else she would start being overwhelmingly familiar with him, which would be equally embarrassing.

Quickly he turned towards Rania.

"Stay here with the General," he whispered.

He then moved away towards Silver as, if they had to have an uncomfortable conversation, the sooner he got it over with the better.

Rania turned to the General.

"Tell me all about what Charles did in the war," she asked. "I have difficulty in making him talk about himself and naturally I am very interested."

"Of course you are, my dear. He was certainly an outstanding soldier. One could always rely on him if things were difficult, or we were in a 'hot spot', there was always Charles! In some ingenious way, he could find a solution to our problems or managed to ensure that we defeated the enemy."

"That is just what I want to hear, General, so please tell me more."

He was just starting rather slowly in his deep voice, when suddenly there was a scream which sounded like that of a dog in pain.

It came from the other side of the railings where the terrace ended, but the bars were so close together that it was almost impossible to see through them.

The dog whined again and Rania heard a man say,

"Can you 'elp us, lady? I finks the poor animal be caught in some-thin'."

Rania thought it was probably caught in a trap and she knew how to release the dog.

During the war when people were so hungry, traps were set in all the woods that belonged to her brother.

When an animal was caught by its leg she would often release it, rather than let it be killed for some-body's supper.

She had often felt rather guilty in doing so, but at the same time she could not bear an animal to suffer.

She rose to her feet as a servant offered the General a drink.

"How can I get to the field outside?" Rania asked the man.

"Just though that door, ma'am, and turn left."

Rania bent towards the General.

"I will not be long. When Charles comes back tell him to join me. I shall be in the field on the other side of these railings with a dog that has been injured."

She did not pause for the General's reply and she hurried inside and found herself in a passage.

Just a little way down it there was a turn to the left as the servant had said.

She ran along to the door at the

end, opened it and stepped out.

She immediately saw two men standing in front of her.

Then a heavy cloth was thrown over her head from behind her.

She felt a rope go around her arms.

At the same time she was lifted off her feet.

She tried to scream, but it was impossible to do so.

The cloth that had been thrown over her head was thick and pulled tightly over her face.

She was being carried, but she had no idea where.

Then she realised with a terrified gasp that she was being kidnapped.

The men were now moving swiftly over the rough ground.

The ropes round her made it impossible for her to move her arms, but as the men stopped for a moment she managed to slip the engagement ring off her finger.

It fell to the ground.

Perhaps, she thought, by a lucky chance, Charles might see it.

Then she was being lowered down onto something and other men were taking her from the two who had been carrying her.

She was thrown roughly down on what appeared to be a hard floor.

Something was moving.

She was being carried away.

She thought despairingly that she would never see Charles again.

Charles reached Silver.

"I have to talk to you, Charles," she insisted.

"There is nothing to talk about."

"I demand that you hear me!"

Charles stiffened.

"Let me make it clear, Silver, that we have nothing to say to each other and nothing to discuss. You told me, if you remember, that you had no wish at all to marry me and handed me back my engagement ring. That, as far as I am concerned, ended our association with each other for ever!"

As Charles finished speaking, he turned away from her to walk back the way he had come.

Silver put out her hand and held on to his arm.

"Wait, Charles, you must listen to

me!"

"No, Silver! From now on we have nothing to say to each other and that is final!"

"You will soon find out that you will change your mind," she retorted.

Charles thought that was a strange thing to say but did not listen.

He merely walked back to where he had left Rania and the General and to his surprise the chair where Rania had been sitting was empty.

"Where is my fiancée?" he asked the General.

"She left me," the old man replied, "because there was a dog in a trap or something and she wanted you to join her."

"A dog in a trap?"

The General made a gesture with his thumb.

"In the field out there."

"I had better go and see what is happening."

Charles walked back into the House of Lords and knowing the layout, he found his way without difficulty.

He opened the door into the field, which was just a rough piece of wasteland with a few trees and nothing else of any consequence.

To his surprise there was no sign of Rania and he wondered where on earth she could be.

Almost automatically he walked towards the river with the terrace where she and the General had been sitting on his left.

Then suddenly he spied something glittering in the grass — it caught the rays of the setting sun.

Without realising what he was doing, he walked to it and bent down to pick it up.

It was Rania's engagment ring!

He stared at it and then at the river.

To his relief he saw there was an old woman sitting under one of the trees nearby with an aged spaniel on a lead.

He hurried towards her.

"Have you by chance seen a young lady here?" he asked. "She was in white and I have just found the ring she was wearing lying near the river."

"I see'd 'er," the old woman replied. "I've never knowed such goings on, that I 'aven't."

"What happened?" Charles asked sharply.

" 'Er comes out of the door over there," she told him pointing with her finger. "Two men there was, waitin' for 'er. One puts a blanket over 'er 'ead. The other two puts ropes around 'er and they takes 'er in their arms."

Charles drew in his breath.

"They took her to a boat?"

"Yes, sir, a big boat 'twas."

"How many men were rowing it?"

"I dunno, but a lot. Perhaps ten or twelve."

"Thank you! Thank you!" cried Charles.

Turning round he started to run and he ran quicker than he had ever run in his life.

He reached the road that ran along the Embankment and increased his speed.

He only had to travel a little over a hundred yards when he saw what he was seeking.

The *Mermaid* was moored where he had told the Captain to wait for them to join it tomorrow morning.

He ran across the ground between the road and his yacht and when he reached it the crew were just about to pull up the gangplank.

Charles sprang on board.

The Captain, who had been checking his men back onto the ship, stared at him in astonishment.

"Cast off at once!" he ordered. "Hurry! There is no time to be lost!"

The men ran to the ropes and he said to the Captain,

"My fiancée has just been kidnapped by men in a galley. It will be sailing downstream and we must overtake it."

The Captain ran to the wheel and Charles followed him.

They were both aware that during the war galleys had proved the most effective method of transport for the smugglers.

The design of these boats was a tribute to the skill, strength and courage of the smugglers and they must have been acutely uncomfortable to handle during the winter.

But with their high speeds they could make a trip to France and back to England in one day.

Only when the *Mermaid* was starting to move away from the river-bank did the Captain ask briefly,

"How many oars?"

"The woman who saw Miss Temple being abducted thought there might have been ten or twelve."

Even as he spoke, he remembered the Captain of a cutter who had pursued galleys during the war, had said,

"It's like sending a cow after a hare!"

To his great relief there was a strong wind which, as all the sails were set, made the *Mermaid* move quicker through the water.

At the same time he was more frightened than he had ever been in his whole life.

It seemed somewhat unlikely they would be able to overtake the galley, which had a good start on them.

He guessed that Rania would have been put in the little cabin which on some of the galleys had been built on their stern.

It was really little more than a cupboard and it was used to carry safely the more delicate articles for which the smugglers found eager purchasers in England.

Silk, lace, velvet and satin ribbons were the articles that almost every woman craved.

Rania weighed so very little and she would hardly slow them down.

Their lightness and length, which made the galleys faster during the war than a cutter under sail, gave them a tremendous advantage.

The *Mermaid* was entirely dependent on the wind, but a galley could move at a high speed with no wind to help.

The Naval authorities had attempted to cope with the galleys and their trade by prohibiting the building of boats with more than six oars all along the coast nearest to France.

But the law had never been effective.

Now there was peace and the smugglers could no longer make a fortune by just crossing the Channel.

The gang, now quite obviously engaged by Silver to rid herself of Rania, must have been delighted at being able to make use of their boat again.

Standing in the bow of the *Mermaid,* Charles held a pair of binoculars to his eyes and looked down river.

It was fortunate that it was summer and the sun was slow to sink and he could see clearly down the Thames for quite a long distance.

The *Mermaid* was in the middle of the river where the tide was stronger and the wind coming from astern was making her move faster.

Even so Charles was thinking

despairingly that if the galley reached the open sea it would be impossible to see it once it was dark.

He had no idea where the kidnappers were heading and at the back of his mind he held the terrifying report he had heard in White's Club.

It was that there was now a new brisk trade being undertaken by the no longer busy smugglers.

They were kidnapping and trafficking English girls into Holland and France to fill the brothels.

'I have to save Rania! I have to save her,' Charles was urging himself over and over again.

The river was growing wider and he knew that soon they would be off Tilbury and then the galley would move into the open sea.

They had only been sailing for a short while, but it seemed to him more like a thousand years.

Then he spied far away in the distance through his binoculars what looked like a galley being rowed down the centre of the river.

It was then that he went below.

One of the stores he had been wise enough to take on board was guns and plenty of ammunition as there were always stories about private boats being held up by pirates.

There were also, wherever they anchored, prowling thieves who would steal anything they could sell.

Charles was not below for long and then came up on deck with six shotguns and two pistols.

He handed a pistol to the Captain, who took it from him without comment.

He thrust the other one into his belt and put down the shotguns.

"You know which of your men are good shots?"

The Captain nodded.

Now they were sailing nearer to the galley Charles had seen in the distance.

He had been right in thinking that there would be a cabin in the stern and that was where they would have put Rania.

Still the galley was a good way from the *Mermaid* and then the fervent prayers Charles was crying out within himself were answered.

A large coal-barge was moving from one side of the Thames to the other. It was slow, large and unwieldy.

Seeing it ahead there was nothing the galley could do but pull over onto the side of the river which the barge was leaving.

Both the Captain and Charles drew in their breath.

They knew this was their big opportunity.

Both of them were aware that while they needed to stop the galley from proceeding, they must not capsize it in doing so.

If they did, Rania would undoubtedly be drowned in the cabin.

Next the galley was moving nearer and nearer to the bank of the river, trying to get through behind the coal-barge.

It was then that the Captain thought that there was just enough room if he moved quickly.

He steered the *Mermaid* up beside the galley and they were almost touching it when a smuggler screamed,

"Look out there! Where the hell d'you think you're goin'?"

It was at that moment that Charles, who had armed the six seamen the Captain had recommended, acted.

They all leaned over the rails overlooking the galley.

Charles in the voice in which he

had given so many orders in the war, shouted,

"Throw your oars overboard!"

For several heart-stopping moments the smugglers hesitated. Then as they saw six guns pointed at them, they reluctantly dropped their oars into the water.

"Hold your arms high above your heads!" ordered Charles. "Any man who drops his arms or tries to escape will be shot."

Being physically very fit he had no difficulty in climbing down from the *Mermaid* into the galley.

"What do you all think you're a-doing?" one of the smugglers screamed.

Charles did not deign to answer.

He ran to the cabin at the stern

of the galley where he knew Rania would be imprisoned.

He was not mistaken and when he pulled open the door he saw her lying on the floor.

The blanket was no longer over her head, but she was gagged and her arms were bound.

He picked her up in his arms and carried her out.

Two seamen leant down from the *Mermaid* to take her as Charles lifted her up and they had hardly pulled her on aboard before he joined them, having clambered with agility up the side of the yacht and onto the deck.

He took Rania from them, ordering,

"Keep those men with their hands

up until I come back!"

He went below, hurried down the companionway, along the passage and into the Master Cabin.

He could feel Rania trembling all over.

He laid her gently down on the bed, undid the gag and untied her.

"Y-you — c-came!" she managed to murmur, almost incoherently. "Oh, C-Charles, you came — *for me*!"

"It is alright, my darling," he told her. "This will never happen again."

She put up her arms as if to hold on to him.

"You are safe here, but I have to get rid of those devils. Then I will come back to you."

He bent his head and his lips met

hers.

Then before she could say another word he had run from the cabin and up on deck.

The six seamen were still pointing their shotguns at the gang of smugglers, who were seated in the galley just as Charles had left them with their hands above their heads.

"I am letting you off lightly," he shouted. "If I ever hear of you again kidnapping an English girl and taking her to a foreign country, I shall make certain you are hanged."

He paused a moment and then added sharply,

"Now get out of the boat and be very thankful you are alive and I am not sending you to prison."

The men scrambled quickly out of the boat.

As soon as they were all on the riverbank Charles ordered the sailors,

"Sink it!"

They all shot into the hull of the galley and holed it.

It slowly filled with up water and only when it had sunk completely did Charles realise that his Captain was waiting for his instructions.

"We will sail back into Tilbury docks, Captain, and thank you for what I think was a tremendous effort on the part of you and your men. I am eternally grateful."

He did not wait for the Captain to reply, but ran below.

He hurried to the Master Cabin,

thinking he would find Rania waiting for him and probably in tears.

He opened the door.

She was lying just as he had left
her with her head on the pillow.

When he reached her side, he saw
she was sound asleep.

He knew it was the sleep of utter
exhaustion such as happened so
often to soldiers during the war.

After a long battle when they had
risked their lives, they would pass
out completely and become oblivi-
ous of everything that was happening around them.

He stood still looking down at
Rania, thinking how lovely she was.

Her fair hair was framing her face
and her long eyelashes were dark
against the transparency of her

skin.

He guessed that being so intelligent, she must have been aware of what the smugglers intended to do with her.

Although she was so very innocent, she would have some idea of where they would be taking her and of what fate awaited her.

He could not imagine that any other woman he had ever encountered would not at this moment be screaming hysterically and clinging to him, utterly out of self-control.

Rania just lay there, looking like a fallen flower.

And fast asleep!

He thought no one could ever be more beautiful and he stood looking at her for a long time.

Then, as he realised how deeply she was asleep, he very gently took off both her shoes and covered her with a bedspread.

As he was doing so he was sending up a prayer of gratitude to God that he had been able to save her.

In only another twenty minutes or certainly in half an hour, they would have been out in the open sea.

Once darkness had come they would have lost sight of the galley and he would never have seen Rania again.

He himself had brought all this on her through their pretend engagement.

Next as he looked again at Rania he wondered what Silver would do next.

He knew from his long experience that *'Hell hath no fury like a woman scorned!'*

Silver had no use now for the unpleasant and boring son of a Duke and she would try in every possible way to coax him back into her clutches.

Charles knew that he could fight for himself — that was no problem, but how could he ever prevent this sort of thing happening perhaps again and again to Rania?

Then he thought that he was being very stupid as of course he knew the answer to his question and as he was aware of what the solution was, he felt as if a heavy burden had slipped from his shoulders.

He looked down at Rania again.

Then very gently his lips touched hers.

She did not wake.

Yet he felt a quiver surge through her as it surged through him at the very same moment.

'I will never lose you again, my darling Rania,' he vowed silently and left the cabin.

CHAPTER SEVEN

Rania woke up and opened her eyes.

For one moment she could not think where she was, and what was happening.

A sudden flash of terror struck her.

She had been abducted by men in a galley and then she realised that now she was no longer in their boat.

There was a small night light burning on the table in a small basin.

For a moment she felt bewildered and then looking up she saw the moonlight coming in through a porthole.

Charles had saved her!

She was aboard the *Mermaid* and she was safe.

She felt the wonder of her escape sweep over her.

She closed her eyes again just in case she had been mistaken.

She was safe! She was safe!

Charles had carried her in his arms and kissed her.

As she thought of his kiss a strange feeling she had never known before seemed to sweep through her body.

She knew it came from her heart.

She loved him. *Of course she loved him!*

She had loved him for a long time and been afraid to admit it even to herself.

He did not love her, but he had kissed her.

She felt fervently that the wonder of his kiss would be something she would remember all through her life.

Then she became aware that she was wearing the evening gown in which she had gone to the party.

She recalled Charles putting her down gently on the bed. He had told her she was safe and he would return.

When he had come, she was asleep.

He must have taken off her shoes and covered her with the bed-spread.

This had all happened before the sun went down and now it was night.

As she had been asleep, Rania thought that Charles must now be asleep too.

She climbed out of bed and managed to undo her gown with some difficulty, putting it down on a chair.

Now that she could see better in the very dim light, she saw that the cabin door was open.

She moved towards it in her stockings, not making a sound.

She looked outside and could see that the door of the cabin next to hers was also open.

That was where Charles must be sleeping.

She peeped into the cabin.

He too had a light in a bowl. It was on the dressing table, not beside his bed.

Nevertheless she could see that he was in bed and asleep.

She went back to her own cabin.

She was safe!

Charles was guarding her and no one could snatch her away from him.

She slipped off her petticoat and got back into bed and almost as soon as she put her head on the pillow, she fell fast asleep again.

This time she was dreaming of Charles.

■ ■ ■ ■

Charles woke early as he always did.

He realised he had slept through the night without being interrupted.

He had expected that Rania would sleep for a long time yet as that was what his soldiers had done in Spain.

He put on a robe which was lying over a chair and walked to the Master Cabin.

When he looked inside he could see at a glance that Rania was still asleep.

He was thinking that it was the best thing that could have happened as it would help her recover from the shock of the horrors she had been through.

Then he noticed her white gown on the chair and he knew she must have been up during the night.

She had not woken him, which meant she had not been afraid.

He closed the door of the Master Cabin very quietly and returned to his own cabin.

He dressed himself and walked into the Saloon to ask for breakfast.

It was still very early, but the seamen were already moving about on deck and he knew that the Captain was getting ready to sail down the river towards the sea.

When he had finished breakfast, Charles went back to his cabin and thought he would again see if Rania was awake.

It was only just after eight o'clock and he knew that because they had been attending so many late parties these past weeks, she had risen early only when they were going riding.

'Perhaps I had better wake her before we move out of the harbour,' he thought to himself.

Then a Steward approached him.

"There be a gentleman to see you, sir, he be in the Saloon."

Charles wondered who it could possibly be.

As he walked into the Saloon he saw a man who he vaguely remembered and for a moment he could not put a name to him.

The man turned from the porthole and holding out his hand, he said,

"Good morning, Charles. Do you remember me?"

Charles stared at him and then exclaimed,

"Walter Althorn! Of course I remember you! What are you doing here?"

Walter Althorn had been the art teacher at Eton.

He had left after three years and became one of the most distinguished designers and restorers of old houses in the country.

He had become what was at the time an overnight sensation in the *Beau Monde* and had been responsible for redecorating Lyndon House in Berkeley Square.

Charles had always been fond of him, but had not seen him for a long time.

"I have read about your yacht in the newspapers," Walter was saying, "and when I happened to see it here in the harbour, I wondered if you had any work for me."

"My yacht has just come in from having some new gadgets added to it, but I cannot believe you are interested in anything so small and unimportant as a yacht."

Walter gave him a wry smile.

"I am interested in anything that would earn me a little money," he confessed. "To be honest Charles, I am at this moment completely broke!"

Charles stared at Walter in amazement and then he realised that he was looking very thin and lined.

"I have just finished breakfast and if you have not had yours I will send for some."

"I would be very grateful, Charles. I have just come from London and as it happens, I am extremely hungry."

He called for the Steward and ordered a substantial breakfast for his guest and as they sat down, he said,

"Do tell me your hard-luck story. I suppose I know the answer to it before you tell me — the war!"

Walter nodded.

"Of course it is the war. Nobody would spend any money with decorators and slowly I was forgotten. I came down to Tilbury because there are often small things to be done to ships calling into the port."

"I cannot imagine you wasting your talent on such trivialities," remarked Charles.

"It provides me with food."

"You said you had just come from London. Were you looking for a job there?"

"No! That is a different story," answered Walter.

He gave a deep sigh before he continued,

"You might as well hear the whole dismal tale. I fell in love!"

"It is something that happens to all of us sooner or later, Walter!"

"She is very pretty and actually I went to London to arrange a Special Marriage Licence, which you may know costs twenty pounds."

"So you are going to be married?"

"I was, but when I got back here half-an-hour ago, I went to my girl's house to be met by her father, who has always disliked me."

"What happened?"

"Because her father had refused to accept me as his son-in-law, we planned to elope, which was why I had to go to London for a Special Licence."

"And the girl's father found out that was what you were doing?" Charles murmured.

"He not only found out, but whilst I was away he forced my fiancée to sail off with someone she disliked and who had been after her for some time. He was leaving for India."

"India!" exclaimed Charles.

"They are to be married at sea by the Captain and as her father told me in no uncertain terms, there is nothing I can do about it and he then kicked me out of his house!"

"I am sorry, Walter, very sorry for you."

"I am sorry for myself. I have no money and we would have had to live on the little that my girl has of her own. Yet somehow I think I would have got back into the world where I was once well-known, so we planned to go to London."

There was much pain in his voice and an expression of agony in his eyes and Charles knew how bitterly he was suffering.

Walter had told him his story directly and without ornamentation, which made his plight even more poignant.

"I am sorry to bore you with my troubles, Charles, and I only called in to see you in case you had some work I could do."

Charles was silent for a moment and then he said,

"I do indeed have a big job for you and one I know you will enjoy."

He saw Walter's eyes light up.

At just that moment the Steward entered and set his breakfast down on the table in front of his chair. He took the silver cover from the plate on which there were eggs, bacon and several sausages.

"Eat your breakfast, Walter, and then I will tell you what I have in store for you."

He walked out of the Saloon to find the Captain.

"I was just coming to see you, sir. I was wondering what time you wanted us to move off."

"I would have said immediately, but I now have a guest, Captain, so I must wait for him to leave and actually there is no hurry."

"I am so looking forward, sir, to showing you how, with its new improvements, the *Mermaid* can go faster than she has ever done before."

"I think you proved that last night, Captain."

"We certainly taught those smugglers a lesson they will not forget in a hurry!"

When Charles went back to the Saloon, Walter had eaten everything on the tray and was finishing his coffee.

"Thank you, Charles, I am very grateful."

Charles sat down in the chair beside him.

"What I want you to do," he now began, "is to go to Temple Hall. Do you remember Harry Temple at Eton?"

"Of course I can remember him well. You two were inseparable."

"We still are, but Harry, like so many other people in the war, has let his house become a shambles compared to its original state."

He saw Walter's eyes light up as he guessed where this conversation was leading him.

"What I would like you to do is to go there at once and restore the house to exactly as it was originally when Harry's father and mother were alive."

He paused a moment before he continued,

"It was, I think, one of the most beautiful houses of the Elizabethan period in England.

"I am paying for it, so money is no object. Make it the perfection that you managed with so many great houses before I joined Wellington's Army."

Walter stared at him.

"I cannot believe what I am hearing," he mumbled.

His voice broke on the last words.

He rose and walked towards a porthole and Charles knew he was fighting back tears that had come into his eyes.

He fully understood that Walter was thinking how exciting it was to be given by him the type of job at which he always excelled.

He noticed a newspaper was lying on the chair that Walter had just left. He must have bought it in London.

Charles picked it up, saw it was *The Morning Post* and opened it.

On the second page he saw his own name in a small paragraph which Walter could easily have overlooked.

It read,

<u>*"Death of the Earl of Lyndonmore*</u>

We deeply regret to report the news that the Earl of Lyndonmore has suffered a fatal accident when out riding yesterday.

His young horse was frightened by a wild dog and bolted into a wood.

The Earl found it impossible to control the animal and when the horse plunged into some trees a bough struck him on the forehead and swept him onto the ground.

His back was broken and he died instantly.

The Earl, who is the seventh holder of the ancient title celebrated his sixty-fifth birthday just two months ago.

He will be very much missed in the

County and his family are being informed of the tragedy of his death."

Charles read it carefully and drew in his breath.

He suspected that the information would have been sent to him immediately at Berkeley Square.

He had already recognised last night that the only effective way he could save Rania from Silver would be if they were married.

He had realised, when he looked down at her asleep and had touched her lips, that he loved her as he had never loved any woman in his life.

But he had been fighting against admitting it.

He was fighting what he had known within himself was a losing battle.

Now he accepted two most important issues.

Firstly that Silver would do anything to prevent him from marrying Rania.

Secondly that it would be quite impossible for him to marry her for several months, even if he suggested that it should be a quiet wedding.

His family would be shocked at such a suggestion when he was in deep mourning for his uncle and it would make it much worse that his uncle had died in such tragic circumstances.

Charles folded up the newspaper and put it into the waste-paper basket by his desk.

Then as Walter turned from the porthole, he said,

"I have another job for you, if it is possible. And it has to be undertaken immediately."

"What is it, Charles?" enquired Walter wiping his eyes with the back of his hand as he walked back to the chair where he had been sitting.

"Do you still have the Special Marriage Licence on you or have you thrown it away?"

"It is right here in my pocket, Charles."

"Good! Then your first job is to change the names for me."

Walter stared at him.

"Change the names?"

"It is a very long story and I will

not bore you with the details. I have here with me someone I want to marry and, for reasons I would rather not discuss, it is important it should take place immediately."

Walter withdrew the Special Licence from the inner pocket of his coat.

"Here it is, Charles, and as you already know it is no longer of any use to me."

"I will give you the money you paid for it, and as well I will give you a letter to my secretary at Berkeley Square who will arrange for any sum you require to be paid at once into your bank. He will also pay every bill for the workmen, materials and everything else that you order."

Walter put the Special Licence in front of Charles on the writing desk.

With a glance he could see that there would be no difficulty, especially if the change in names was completed by Walter's brilliant hands.

He rose from his chair and Walter sat down.

"If you were being married today," asked Charles, "was the Church here in Tilbury?"

"Yes, St. Mary's. It is a nice little Church with a charming old Vicar whom I have known for years. He was let into the reason why we had to be married secretly."

"At what time was this ceremony to take place?"

"We had planned it as soon as I got back. I would call for Alice, thinking her father would have left for his office."

"Instead he was waiting for you."

"He was so delighted to humiliate me!"

"It is something you will not regret when the work you do at Harry's house and later at Lyndon Hall will put you back on the pedestal, which you have always graced so brilliantly."

"I just want to believe every word you are saying," replied Walter. "But for the moment I find it difficult."

"Alter the Special Licence for me," urged Charles, "and then you shall take me to your Vicar and I am asking you as an old friend to act as my Best Man."

"You are the best friend I have ever had," Walter muttered softly.

Charles left him to work on the Special Licence and went below.

He knocked gently on the door of the Master Cabin and heard Rania call out,

"Come in."

When he entered the cabin, Charles found she was not only awake but had dressed herself in the white gown she had worn last night.

For a moment they just stood looking at each other.

Then with a little cry she threw herself against him.

"You saved me. How can I — ever

thank you? You saved me! When all I wanted to do — was to *die!*"

Charles put his arms around her.

And then without saying a word he was kissing her wildly, demandingly, possessively.

He knew that his overwhelming desire to kiss her was because he was afraid he had lost her.

And his love, which he had kept suppressed for so long, was no longer under his control.

To Rania it was as if the skies had opened.

He was carrying her up into the sunshine and they were in a Heaven of their own.

Charles raised his head.

"Now please tell me," he said in a voice which was slightly unsteady, "what you feel for me."

"*I love you,* Charles. I love you! When I thought I would never see you again, I did not want to go on living!"

"I don't think I have ever suffered such agonies in my life when I realised what had happened to you."

"But you saved me!" she sighed. "How can you be so wonderful — so clever?"

He kissed her again before she could say any more, then raising his head, he said,

"There is no time to waste!"

"Where are w-we going?"

Her voice too was unsteady because of her love.

"We are going to be married."

Rania's eyes opened wide.

"Married?"

"I am not taking any further risks that you will run away from me or be eaten up by sharks in the sea, my dear darling. So we are to be married by a Special Licence as soon as we reach a Church here in Tilbury."

Rania drew in her breath.

"It will be a very small and quiet wedding," Charles told her. "Do you mind that?"

"How could I mind anything just as long as I can be with you for ever? I was so terrified that the day would come when you would no longer want me as your pretend fiancée and I would have to go back to the country alone."

"That will never ever happen and

you will never be alone," he promised. "You may not be able to do without me, but I cannot do without *you*!"

He kissed her again and then suggested,

"Come with me to the Saloon to meet the man who has arranged our marriage for us."

Rania wondered how this could be possible, but she asked no questions.

As Charles took her hand in his, she said,

"Could you please first do up the back of my dress? It was difficult last night to undo it and now I find I cannot fasten the top buttons."

Charles chuckled.

"I expect I shall have to do this

many times in the future!"

He did up her buttons and kissed the back of her neck.

Hand in hand he took her along to the Saloon where Walter had just finished altering the Special Licence.

He rose as they entered and Charles said to Rania,

"Let me introduce you, darling, to Walter Althorn, who is the most brilliant designer and restorer of houses in the whole country."

He smiled at Walter as he continued,

"As soon as we are married he is leaving at once for Temple Hall, which he is going to restore to all its former glory as a surprise present for Harry."

Rania gave a cry of delight.

"Oh, Charles, only you could think of something so wonderful! It will be so marvellous for Harry to go back to when he has finished with your Racecourse."

"I thought it would please you, dearest Rania, but now Walter is going to take us to St. Mary's Church where the Parson is waiting for us."

Rania wondered just how it had all been arranged so quickly, but she was far too happy to ask any questions.

Then she gave a little cry.

"If I am to be married, I must have a veil. I cannot walk into the Church with nothing on my head."

She had succeeded, just before

Charles joined her, to brush and pin up her hair in much the same fashion that Antonio had done it last night.

Now she thought if they could find a veil, it would hide any discrepancies.

To her surprise Walter put his hand in his pocket.

"It is with the possible greatest pleasure," he spoke up triumphantly, "that I can give you a wedding present!"

He handed Rania a small parcel and she wondered what it could be.

She took off the tissue paper and she saw that it was a veil made of very soft tulle.

"I am afraid this veil has not been in my family for generations, but it will serve its purpose," Walter told her.

"Of course it will," agreed Rania, shaking it, "and all I need to keep it in place are two flowers to pin it down on each side over my ears."

"We will stop on our way to the Church," Charles suggested.

He ordered the Steward to call for a carriage and it must be the best one available, and then as the man hurried away he went on deck to speak with the Captain, who was standing on the bridge impatient to move the *Mermaid* out of harbour.

"My plans have now somewhat changed, Captain," he began. "I am to be married immediately and I would like you to take us on quite a prolonged honeymoon!"

The Captain stared at him, thinking he was joking.

He thought for a second and then burst out,

"My heartiest congratulations, sir, I had no idea —"

"We will talk about it another time. What I want you to do now is to stock up the ship with all the food and provisions you will require right away. We will, of course, stop at various French ports on the way and then at Lisbon before we reach Gibraltar and the Mediterranean."

He saw the delight on the Captain's face and there was no need for him to put his feelings into words.

"I expect we shall be ready to put to sea in about an hour-and-a-half," said Charles, walking away.

He heard the Captain giving sharp orders before he reached the Saloon to rejoin Rania and Walter.

"Everything is arranged," he told them, "and while I write a note for you, Walter, to take to Major Monsell in Berkeley Square, Rania must now make a list of what she requires immediately for a *long* sea voyage."

"I have nothing!" she cried. "Nothing but what I'm wearing now!"

"I know, darling, as soon as we are married Walter can take us, I am sure, to a local shop where you can buy a few essentials and then we can stop for more in France."

He smiled at her lovingly before

he finished,

"We shall also stop everywhere else for what will eventually be, I promise you, a very exquisite trousseau."

He thought Rania might protest that he was asking too much of her.

Instead she laughed.

"Only you, Charles, could think of marrying a bride who has nothing to wear but a white evening gown and a veil which was our first wedding present!"

"I am certain that the French will be able to frame you even better than the English have done, Rania!"

His eyes were twinkling and she knew that he was enjoying his surprises for her.

She was quite sure that in his own magical way she would get everything she wanted and a great deal more.

'I love him,' she said to herself. 'No man could be more magnificent or more exciting.'

The carriage was waiting for them at the quay and Charles had a last word with the Captain.

Then they drove off to the small and ancient little Church on the outskirts of the town of Tilbury

Because it appeared so unpretentious, Charles could understand why Walter had chosen this Church for his runaway wedding.

The Parson was old and kindly and he might have thought it odd that Walter was not to be married while his friend was, but he was too tactful to say so.

There were white flowers on the altar and down the aisle.

He read the Marriage Service with great sincerity.

Rania considered that it could not have been a more moving and memorable service if it had taken place in a Cathedral.

There had been no time at all for Charles to buy her a wedding ring, so he drew his signet ring from his finger and although it was a little large for her, Rania felt it was a potent symbol of their love.

As the old Parson blessed them, Charles and Rania were both thinking of the love they had talked about.

Charles had believed it was impossible to find this very special love and yet he knew now he had really found it and it was even more perfect than he had longed for.

For Rania the Marriage Service was so incredibly beautiful and so perfect she felt as if it came to her from Heaven itself.

She knew she would have hated a big wedding with hundreds of guests she did not know and who were not any part of her life.

She would have loved Harry to be there, but she felt he would understand.

When the service was over they thanked the Parson and Charles gave him a generous donation for the Church.

Then as the three of them got back into the carriage Charles said to Walter,

"Now we must go shopping, and next we must be away on our honeymoon — and the sooner you reach London and settle matters with Major Monsell, the sooner you will forget your own problems."

He realised that it must have been very painful for Walter to see him and Rania taking his place in front of the altar, but he hoped that once Walter was back working in the world where he had been so successful he would find someone very special to marry himself.

Walter then took them to the most fashionable and he added 'and most expensive shop' in

Tilbury.

Rania managed to quickly find two day dresses she could wear on the yacht and a coat and cape in case it was cold as well as two nightgowns, a negligee, stockings and several other necessities.

Charles had wandered away whilst Rania's clothes were being packed up and when he returned to the shop he was holding a small parcel in his hand which she guessed was a present.

But she was too wise to ask him any questions.

They all drove back to the *Mermaid,* but Walter did not come aboard with them as Charles had made it clear that he should go at once to London.

He ordered a Hackney Carriage for him and it drew up at the end of the quay before they had said goodbye to each other.

"If you are in any difficulties at our home," Rania said to Walter, "you know where Harry is. Only we want to keep this a secret surprise for as long as possible."

"Leave it all to me. I have not yet had time to tell you that I once met both your parents and thought how charming they were. Therefore it seems a greater pleasure, even than it would have been anyway, to do something for the home where you and Harry were brought up."

"It makes everything seem even more amazing for us too," she replied.

Walter took Charles's hand.

"I have no words to tell you how I feel and what I am thinking. I can only know, having seen Rania, that God has blessed you."

"He has indeed," answered Charles. "So hurry up, Walter, and get to work. By the time I return I expect to find several more jobs for you!"

He was thinking as he spoke of the other houses his uncle owned which he would now inherit.

None of them were by any means as magnificent as Lyndon Hall, but there was a manor house at Newmarket where Charles had every intention of keeping some of his horses. There was also a small castle in Scotland where his uncle used to go grouse shooting in the autumn.

Walter would handle all of them, Charles thought, and they should keep him busy and prosperous.

"I wish you both every possible happiness in the world," proposed Walter. "I know instinctively that you are made for each other."

"That is just the nicest thing you could say," sighed Rania and she bent forward and kissed him on the cheek.

"When you are in London, please will you pat my horse Dragonfly and tell him that I am thinking of him."

"I have given orders for Dragonfly and two of my horses to go to the country," Charles intervened. "So when we return home we will find them at Lyndon Hall."

Rania smiled at him.

"You think of everything, Charles, and I have said that to you before."

"I am only thinking of you, my darling."

They walked onboard, the gangplank was pulled up and they waved to Walter on the quay.

When they were saying goodbye, all the items they purchased in the shops had been taken down to the Master Cabin.

Rania was astonished to find that whilst they were being married, the Master Cabin of the *Mermaid* had been redecorated on Charles's orders.

He had ordered only white flowers, but such a large quantity could not be found. There were therefore pink roses, carnations and all the flowers of spring.

Rania looked at Charles.

"Now I really do feel like a bride," she murmured.

"*I* will make certain that you feel a bride as well a little later, Rania, but I want you to open the first of many wedding presents."

He put the little package he had bought in the shop into her hands.

"What is in it?" Rania asked intrigued.

"Look and you will see, my darling."

She opened it quickly to find a little velvet box that contained a wedding ring.

"This is a symbol," he told her, "that you are mine for eternity and though I forgot the ring before we reached the Church, it is something I will never forget again."

He took off the signet ring they had been married in and then put the wedding ring on her finger.

It fitted her exactly.

"It is a lovely present and one I will never lose."

"Just as I will never lose you," added Charles. "You are mine, my dearest darling, and I am the luckiest man in the world to have you as my wife."

"I do remember you saying over and over again that you did not want to be married, so I shall have to try very hard to prevent you being bored with me."

"I could never be bored with you, Rania. I had no intention of getting married because I had never fallen in love. Now I am so completely and utterly in love and it is quite different from anything I have ever felt before."

"Are you sure of that?" she asked him.

"Quite, quite sure! I love you, my precious darling, in a thousand different ways I have never felt or dreamt of. It is so perfect, so glorious, so sublime, I know it can only have come from Heaven."

"That is just what I feel too and when I prayed and prayed that you would save me and you did, I knew that God would never forget us, now or in the future."

They were sitting on the bed as they talked.

Now Charles tipped Rania back against the pillows.

"I love you, I adore you, my darling, and there is so much I have to teach you about love. It will take me not only this lifetime, but perhaps a great number of lives to come."

Rania put her arms around his neck.

"I am a very eager pupil," she whispered, blushing.

Charles kissed her.

As he did so the *Mermaid* started moving out of the port and towards the open sea.

It was as if the soft lap of the

waves was a musical background to everything they were feeling for each other.

Yet this was only the beginning.

Just as the whole world now lay in front of them to explore, so their love was waiting for them to find.

It was a perfect treasure and wonderfully exciting.

As Rania was to agree later, it would be impossible to discover it all in one lifetime.

It would require many more lives before they knew all of what is eternal and inexpressible — except for those who truly seek it.

Charles's lips were holding hers captive.

He kissed her and went on kissing her.

She knew that she would give him her heart and her soul as well as her body.

They would be one person complete in each other.

Nothing and nobody could ever separate them.

"I love you, my glorious precious beautiful one," he was murmuring.

"And I love you and love you with all of me," she answered.

After what seemed a long time later they enjoyed luncheon and now the *Mermaid* was out at sea and moving down the English Channel.

The sun was shining brightly, the sea was smooth and she was sailing swiftly, far swifter than Charles had thought was possible.

He appreciated that his innovations, which included the length and strength of the masts, had surely made the *Mermaid* unique.

She was also supremely comfortable in other ways.

The Chef who had been with Charles for two years was a Frenchman.

At first he had been slightly ashamed of employing an enemy he had fought so strongly against.

Actually the Chef had stayed in England during the war and he had hidden himself in one of Charles's cottages in the country.

He was so pleased to be back at work again that he excelled himself and the meals he cooked for Charles and Rania became more and more delicious.

They had now been sailing for five days and were moving into the Bay of Biscay.

Only then did Charles tell Rania that he was now the Earl of Lyndonmore.

"How do you know?

"Actually I knew before we left England."

Rania looked at him in consternation.

"But you should have attended the funeral!"

"It is just unfortunate that I have fallen in love with a very beautiful young girl. But it was impossible for me to marry her at once, because as the Earl of Lyndonmore, I would have been in deep mourning for my uncle."

"So that is why we had to marry in such a hurry and so secretly?"

"What really scared me was that you might refuse me or escape from me, my darling."

"Or — or be stolen away again!"

"That was indeed the real reason and once you were married, you were now completely and absolutely safe."

"I knew it must have been the girl who refused to marry you who had arranged for me to be kidnapped."

"How do you know that?"

"I heard the man, when he took the blanket off my head, say to the other one, 'she's a tasty bit of goods and she'll fetch us a good price!

With that and the money from the pretty woman we'll be able to buy a new galley'."

Charles did not say anything and Rania continued,

"Of course everybody in London told me they had expected you to marry Silver Bancroft, so I knew it was she who had paid them to carry me away!"

They were lying on the bed while they talked.

Charles put his arms around his wife and pulled her closer to him.

"Forget it all, my loved one."

"Are you quite certain," enquired Rania, "that you have forgotten her? She is very, very attractive."

"A beautiful body with an ugly heart — and that, my precious

Rania, is why you are so different. You are very beautiful, so much more beautiful than anyone I have ever seen. But your heart is as perfect as the sun and the stars."

Rania moved a little closer to him.

"You say such wonderful things to me. I hope you will go on saying them."

"I have only just started. Every day when I look at you and touch you, my precious, I will think of even more and more ways to tell you how much I love you and how happy I am."

"Have I really made you happy, Charles?"

"That is a silly question. You must know that I am happier than I have ever been in the whole of my life."

"And I am so very happy *too,*" she exclaimed, "that sometimes I do feel that it is almost wrong that we should have such happiness when there is so much suffering in the world outside."

"We will help the world whenever we can. That is something in which I know you will guide me."

"You are surely the kindest and the most generous man who ever lived and I cannot imagine anything I could teach you that you do not know already."

Charles moved his hand tenderly down the side of her cheek.

"I did not know until I loved you, Rania, what love meant. I know that when you give me a son, I shall for the first time in my life know what it means to be a father and have children of my own."

He stopped speaking for a short moment to take a long look at Rania.

"One discovers when one is *really* in love which are the issues of greatest importance even while to other people they may seem something quite ordinary."

"Nothing about you, darling Charles, could ever be ordinary!"

"And I can say the same about you."

"If we are both so extraordinary," suggested Rania, "we must do extraordinary things. When we go home we must make quite certain that you are an example to every landlord in the way you look after your tenants and treat the people who work for you."

"I have every intention of doing just that."

"We must attempt to make people on your estate as happy as we are and perhaps, if we are an example to them, we can be an example to others, even those in London."

Charles laughed.

"They are so stuck up and pleased with themselves in London that they think they know about everything, but we know we have found the secret of real happiness and that is what we will try to find for other people."

"It is such a lovely idea. But my darling Charles, I don't want you to have to worry over too many pretty or enchanting women!"

"And I have no intention," he parried, "of allowing you to worry over tall, dark, handsome men!"

"As though I would want to!"

"Whether you want to or not, I intend to be a very jealous husband and I will not have all those bucks running after you and flirting with you in future!"

"It is your fault that they do," she protested. "You dressed me up and made me a beauty!"

"I did it to spite Silver and then I realised that I had the sun, the moon and all the stars in my arms, and it was *you*!"

"That is only where I always want to be, Charles."

Then it became impossible to

speak again because he was kissing her.

He was kissing her and evoking within her a wild, excited ecstasy.

It seemed to flood through them both like the flame from a fire or the light from the sun.

It was the spirit of Love itself which joined them completely.

As Charles made Rania his they were one person.

They were now complete, as the ancient Greeks had believed, and they had found each other once more.

Now they could never be parted.

"I love you! I adore you!" they whispered to each other again and again.

The love they were feeling in their

bodies and souls came down to them just like a burning flame from Heaven above to envelop them in all its glory.

ABOUT THE AUTHOR

Barbara Cartland, who sadly died in May 2000 at the age of nearly 99, was the world's most famous romantic novelist. She wrote 723 books in her lifetime, with worldwide sales of over 1 billion copies and her books were translated into 36 different languages.

As well as romantic novels, she wrote historical biographies, 6 autobiographies, theatrical plays, books of advice on life, love, vitamins and cookery. She also found time to be a political speaker and television and radio personality.

She wrote her first book at the age of 21 and this was called *Jigsaw*. It became an immediate bestseller and sold 100,000 copies in hardback and was translated into 6 different languages. She wrote continuously throughout her life, writing bestsellers for an astonishing 76 years. Her books have always been immensely popular in the United States, where in 1976 her current books were at numbers 1 & 2 in the B. Dalton bestsellers list, a feat never achieved before or since by any author.

Barbara Cartland became a legend in her own lifetime and will be best remembered for her wonderful romantic novels, so loved by her millions of readers throughout the world.

Her books will always be treasured for their moral message, her pure and innocent heroines, her good looking and dashing heroes and above all her belief that the power of love is more important than anything else in everyone's life.

The employees of Thorndike Press hope you have enjoyed this Large Print book. All our Thorndike, Wheeler, and Kennebec Large Print titles are designed for easy reading, and all our books are made to last. Other Thorndike Press Large Print books are available at your library, through selected bookstores, or directly from us.

For information about titles, please call:
(800) 223-1244

or visit our website at:
gale.com/thorndike

To share your comments, please write:
Publisher
Thorndike Press
10 Water St., Suite 310
Waterville, ME 04901